Praise for *Kat's Gree.. ....*

"Family and friendship, especially the nuanced complications of generational love and devotion, are beautifully drawn in *Kat's Greek Summer*. Mima Tipper excels at bringing to life the gentleness and fire of first love, as well as Kat's dawning awareness that only she can stake her own claim in the world. A wise and charming debut."

—ALISON MCGHEE, Pulitzer Prize nominee
and *New York Times* best-selling author of *Shadow Baby*

"relatable . . . sympathetic . . . The prose is detailed and descriptive. In the coming-of-age novel *Kat's Greek Summer*, a girl embraces her Greek identity and begins to understand who she wants to be."

—FOREWARD CLARION REVIEWS

"Meet Kat Baker. She's not the girl you want to be; she's the girl you are. Mima Tipper's impetuous, likable protagonist learns that desire is a wellspring that spurs her forward like Artemis, the goddess she can be if she trusts her instincts and stays true to herself. Readers will love this fresh for-real heroine."

—JULIE PIDGEON, Principal and Middle School English Teacher,
Folsom Education and Community Center, South Hero, Vermont

"*Kat's Greek Summer* is a charming tale of self-discovery, family, and first love set in a vibrant Greek village. With unforgettable characters and a touch of romance, it's a perfect read for fans of heartfelt coming-of-age stories."

—KEAGAN CALKINS, Library Director,
Worthen Library, South Hero, Vermont

KAT'S GREEK SUMMER

KAT'S GREEK SUMMER

A Novel

MIMA TIPPER

SPARKPRESS

Published by SparkPress, a BookSparks imprint,
A division of SparkPoint Studio, LLC
Phoenix, Arizona, USA, 85007
www.gosparkpress.com

Published 2025
Printed in the United States of America
Print ISBN: 978-1-68463-306-7
E-ISBN: 978-1-68463-307-4
Library of Congress Control Number: 2024927041

Interior design and typeset by Katherine Lloyd, The DESK

For our number one *yiayiá*,
my mother Sofia.

CHAPTER ONE

*L*ove the running. *Love it.* Chanting the words in her head like a spell, Kat ran, gritting her teeth, ready to explode, ready to melt, maybe both. *Love, love, love it.* The hot, muggy air of mid-June in Connecticut was the worst, though, making every stride heavy, every breath a drowning gasp. *Keep going. Keep going. Almost there.* Kat wiped sweat from her face as she ran by the high school—*go Rams!*—crossed Farm Road, and, at last, turned onto Shady Hills Road. Huffing and puffing now, she started up the long, sweltering, not-even-close-to-shady incline that led up, up into the neighborhood. *C'mon. Love the running. Love it!* All the running sites said exactly that. And she *would* love the running. Yeah, she would. The second her body got past the hate-the-running phase, because—because that's what she wanted. More than anything. To be the fastest runner. The best.

Kat gulped thick, hot air, cranked up the volume on her music, and ran harder, telling herself to remember *why* she was running. Telling herself to visualize. The sites said that, too. That visualizing was the key to forgetting her bursting lungs, her screaming leg muscles. She had to see her goals, believe her dreams, and, most important of all, keep running. Keep running. One step, another, one step . . .

The pounding of her shoes on the pavement echoed in Kat's head, her gaze fuzzing as she visualized like crazy. About how it would be. How *she* would be. *Yes.*

Cross-country star Kat Baker flies by the pack, legs stretching, breath coming slow and even. She takes the lead, racing down a grassy chute lined with screaming fans, and there, the finish line. Her arms fling back, her chest rips through the tape, and everything goes super slo-mo, hundreds of amazed voices roaring, Did you see her? That freshman broke the high school record! *Dozens of people rush up, clapping her back, giving her high fives. Then, their bodies part, and Mike Doherty, beautiful, golden, and so captain-of-the-boys-team, walks toward her. He puts his hand on her shoulder, looks deep into her eyes, and—*

"Woo-hoo! Here comes the big runnah!"

The loud yelp drilled into Kat, and she stumbled to a stop. Slowly, her surroundings came into focus. House, yard, driveway. James. Little brother and number one fantasy buster. He stood on his skateboard under the open garage door waving at her like a madman.

"Hey, Kat! Guess what?"

Since Kat could hardly catch her breath, much less try to talk, she tossed him a small wave and crossed to the driveway. She had to stop again, though, and press her palm against her chest. Man, her lungs were on fire! She turned off her music and leaned over, hands on her knees now. *Love the running.* The words ran through her head, hot and liquid. *Love it!*

An explosive *vroom* mixing with yells of "Oh, yeah!" and "Bend it, baby!" jerked her around. A car tooled by, the boys inside smirking and pointing. Kat's stomach, already trembly from exertion, went sour, and she couldn't keep herself from yanking at the bottoms of her running shorts. She wanted to answer them in some cool way, but what *was* that way? Frown and wag a finger? Smile and wave? She did nothing, except close the mouth she was pretty sure had been hanging open.

James skated down the drive, fist raised. "Get lost, losers!"

"James!" she hissed. "Shut it!"

"Well, they are."

"Look, I don't want . . ." Kat shook her head. Embarrassing enough that those boys caught her scared-rabbit face, did she honestly have to explain to James that sticking up for her like a mini bodyguard made everything even worse?

"Forget it," she said. She slouched by him and up the driveway.

James called after her, the excitement in his voice catching, but no, Kat didn't stop. She had stuff to do. Important running stuff.

While she walked, Kat dragged her braid over her shoulder, combing her fingers through the tail end. Today she'd run all the way to the Carriage Barn and back, so that had to be at least a mile, and she was getting better, faster. A couple more weeks and she'd be ready to start training with New Canaan High's cross-country team. Then everything would be different. She'd be with the team, no, she'd *belong* to the team, and she'd start to know things. Things about high school, and what to do about boys that, well, she was supposed to start knowing.

She stepped into the cool, dark garage, enjoying a moment of relief before her eyes adjusted. Empty moving boxes and crumpled newspaper littered the floor. Her insides drooped. A gazillion full boxes waited in the house, and now that she had finished her run, Mom would probably ask her to spend the rest of the day unpacking.

She kicked at a box. All that could wait. Right now,

according to her list of top training tips for distance runners, she needed to hydrate.

Making her way to the drinks' fridge in the corner, she tugged open the door and leaned into the chill blast. *What should she have today? Energy? Or maybe . . . yes, definitely, Power.*

She grabbed the neon blue bottle, and there was James again, skating over, wheels screeching.

"So," he said, poking her elbow, "are you ready to 'guess what' now?"

Kat took her time twisting the cap off her drink and downing a long swallow of cold and sweet. That James. He practically quivered, his whole body warring between wanting to tell her his news and wanting to make her ask. Look at him. He wasn't as short as she expected him to be. He'd turned eleven the week before, but since she was almost four years older, she'd always pretty much towered over him. Now she barely had to look down from her lofty five feet, seven and a half inches to meet his eyes. The little creepazoid was getting taller.

"Fine," he said at last, "I won't tell you."

Taller *and* smarter.

"Oh, all right." Kat cracked a tiny smile and lifted her drink again. "What is it?"

James spoke in a rush. "Mom says we're going on a big trip. To Greece. Can you believe it? All the way to Paralia!"

Kat stood, the bottle frozen in her hand. But her mouth must've dropped open, because James snickered in that happy way of having shocked the flaming spank out of his big sister.

CHAPTER TWO

reece? Paralia? What?

Mouth open, ready to yell for Mom, Kat yanked open the door to the mudroom. And stopped cold. No. James had to be confused or—*wait!* Wait. One. Minute. She looked back into the garage. Empty, of course.

That James. Kat almost laughed as she went into the mudroom. How he *loved* messing with her: such a hit-and-run clown. Shutting the door, she hesitated, hand still on the knob. Except, how would *he* know how she felt about Paralia?

She plopped down on the mudroom bench, swigged from her drink. He *wouldn't* know, and now she was being dumb. "Dumb," she said under her breath, and leaned over, untying her shoe. Knowing James, he *wanted* to go to Greece. Why, he and Mom probably spent the whole morning looking at those old Greek photo albums again. *God.* Kat shook her head. Mom was getting so . . . strange. Before the move, she'd been obsessed with those old photos, trying to get both Kat and James to stop packing and sit with her to go through them. She'd gotten worse since they'd been in this new house, too. All her big sighing when they watched TV. Those spacey looks at the dinner table.

Kat tugged off her shoe and shifted to the other foot. Of course, the last couple of years *had* been pretty intense for

Mom. Working super hard to get her teaching certificate. Being forced to sell their big, wonderful house—*their home!*—to move all the way across town to this much smaller, super lame house that wasn't even theirs. Nope. One of Mom's teacher friends was renting it to them. So rugged.

Kat pulled off her other shoe. Sometimes Mom mentioned stuff about Greece, about Yiayiá, but there was no way she would spring a major trip out of the blue.

A low murmur drifted through the entryway to the kitchen. Mom talking and, funny thing, she was speaking Greek. And it was "Greek" to Kat, because she didn't speak more than a couple of token words. Mostly, she forgot Mom was Greek. Dad wasn't Greek. Nothing in their lives was Greek. The only time Kat even noticed the slight chop to Mom's English was when she had a new friend. "Is your mom from, like, Russia? Germany? France?" they'd ask. *Seriously?* Maybe Russia but, come on, Germany? France?

Now Mom's *choppity-chop* Greek floated out to Kat loud and clear.

"*Naí, naí,*" Mom was saying, then a pause. Sounded like she was on the phone. A click of her tongue now, a breathy laugh and, "*Naí,* Mamá—" she had to be talking to Yiayiá Sofia— "*stin* Paralia . . ."

Kat startled. James *hadn't* been messing with her.

"Paralia," Mom repeated, followed by a stream of words, sharp and excited as high heels *tap, tap, tapping.*

Kat leaned her head back against the wall, blurry memories surfacing of the only time they'd visited Paralia. It was right after Grandpa, no, Pappoús Nikita passed away. She was about five—hold up, James had learned to walk by then; she must've been closer to six. It took forever to fly there, and they got stuck in some airport. She remembered Dad bringing over drinks in paper cups. Then he and Mom started arguing in that low whisper that Kat soon learned was them pretending to talk. She saw herself taking a sip of the too-bright, too-orange soda and gagging at the thick, warm, sick-sweet taste.

Kat scrunched up her face now, as though tasting the drink again.

The rest of that trip to Paralia was a haze. Bright white heat. Voices barking words she couldn't understand. Squeezed into a big car, they'd driven away from the Athens airport, way, way out of the city, and up over what must've been a mountain. Kat frowned, her mind going blank.

The car plunged down a long, winding road. She remembered that. Tires crunching hard against gravel and dirt. By the time they reached the bottom, she was majorly carsick. She tried to picture Paralia—the village, the harbor—but all her mind could see were white and gray and black pebbles, and her younger self barfing up orange goo. Dad was angry; Mom was too quiet. They both stayed that way for a long time. Dad didn't want to be there, and there was nothing Mom could do to change his mind. He didn't want to be in that tiny fishing village full of heat, dust, and Greeks. Paralia.

Mom's loud, bright *"Entáxei"* snapped Kat back, the high-fiving Greek "all right" a reminder of James's glee in the garage.

Blowing out a long breath, Kat stared down at her feet covered in sweat-grimed socks. Okay, *fine*. They were going to Greece. To Paralia. Change of plans. She'd miss one, maybe two weeks of summer training, but that could be good. She'd go to the beach, get a killer tan. A flutter of excitement hit her belly, and she grabbed both of her running shoes, hugging them tight on her lap. On top of looking great, she'd have something awesome to talk about when she showed up for cross-country practice. *Perfect.*

Kat buzzed through her "keep your running shoes running" checklist, slipped her brushed-off and aired-out shoes under the bench, and strolled into the kitchen. Instantly, the buttery smell of a freshly toasted bagel made her mouth water. She'd wanted to get out running the moment she woke up that morning and had skipped breakfast. Probably why she missed the big travel news.

Mom sat at the breakfast table surrounded by unpacked boxes and bins. She was off the phone now and hunched over her laptop, humming. Mom was cheery all right, and more excited than Kat had seen her in a long time. Shifting to pick up her bagel, she caught sight of Kat and her smile grew.

"Hi, sweets. Good run? Did you make it to Waveny Park?"

"Yeah, all the way to the Carriage Barn," Kat said, then angled her head. "So . . . Paralia? Seriously?"

"Oh, did James tell you already? I wanted it to be a surprise."

"Yeah, he told me," Kat said. She moved around the kitchen, rustling up what she needed for a big bowl of cereal. "And don't worry, I'm surprised all right." She let out a small laugh, tapping the cereal box against a big bin sitting on the counter. "Pretty sudden, considering the big move."

"I know this might *seem* sudden," said Mom, "but I've been thinking of taking you and James to Greece for a long time." She gestured toward the bins as if they were old friends. "We've already unpacked most of what we need. We can take our time with the rest. Yiayiá is thrilled we want to come." Her shining eyes widened.

"Okay, I get it, 'Let's go!'" finished Kat, joining Mom at the table. "Still, you could've said something earlier." Lifting her brimming spoon to her mouth, she froze. "Wait." She studied Mom's face, a finger of worry poking at her. "You're not . . . sick or anything."

"No. God, no!"

"Is Yiayiá sick?"

"No. Goodness—such drama. It's nothing of the kind. We are simply long, *long* overdue for a trip to Greece is all, and I can't wait . . ."

With Mom's enthusiastic chatter filling her ears, Kat ate, her gaze drifting to the laptop, taking in the blue-and-white logo reading *HellasAir*. She frowned at the screen. "You made a mistake there," she said, pointing with her spoon.

Mom broke off midsentence, twisting to look. "What?"

"The flight stuff. You put an 8 instead of a 6. For the dates."

"No. That's right. Departing June 15 and returning August 25."

"What?" Kat's hand sagged to the table, the spoon she'd used as a pointer clattering on the wood. "You want to spend the *summer* there? The *whole* summer?"

"Of course." Mom's smile bloomed. "Won't that be wonderful?"

"But—but—" *Was Mom kidding?* "We can't go for the whole summer."

"Why not? It'll be fantastic. We can really settle into the cottage." Mom hesitated, her forehead wrinkly with confusion. "I was sure you'd be over the moon about this trip. James is."

"I—I—" Kat swallowed hard. What about *her* plans? What about the team? "I'm fine with going. Only not for the whole summer."

"I don't understand," Mom murmured. "I thought you would be excited to spend the summer in Greece. Get to know

Yiayiá better. Your cousins." She gazed up at Kat, her eyes full of a need Kat had never seen before. "Please, Katina."

Kat stared into the dregs of her cereal. She didn't like it when Mom used her full name, the sound of it an itch in her head she couldn't scratch. And she had no problem "getting to know" Yiayiá and the cousins, but that didn't mean she wanted to move in with them for the summer.

"It's just"—Kat made herself look right at Mom—"I really, really want to stay in New Canaan this summer. C'mon, Mom, it's the summer before I start high school."

Mom's expectant face urged her to spill her plan.

"I want to do cross-country in the fall. The team starts summer training soon and I can, you know, run with them and—"

"All right. Slow down." Mom studied Kat. "Cross-country sounds like a great idea, but . . ."

There it was—Mom's "I sound like I'm listening, but I'm not" tone.

"I'm sure you can join the team when school starts." Mom reached to give Kat's hand a quick pat. "Greece is very important to me, to *us*, and I want us to go. We never have."

"That's not true," Kat said, the words stinging her throat. "We went there when I was six. With Dad."

Mom breathed in sharply as their eyes met. "You were very young. I—I cannot believe you remember that."

"Well, I do."

Mom's face, no longer happy and smiling, made Kat clamp her lips shut. Hard as she pressed them together, she couldn't stop them from trembling.

"I am sad that's what you remember," Mom said finally, her shoulders slumping as she turned to the computer screen again. "But the plans are made. We leave in three days."

CHAPTER THREE

The car jerked as if it wanted to leap up the narrow mountain road, and all Kat could think was that in the years since the one and only time she'd done this drive to Paralia, nothing had changed. Not the chalky whiteness of the road, or the dust billowing out behind the car. Not the pale un-blue sky, or the sun biting through the car windows.

The ground spread up a dry, rocky slope covered with scrubby bushes and—*were those goats?* Yes, two brown-and-white goats meandered near the road, their jaws working and working, oblivious both to the cloud of dust raised by the car and to the shimmers of heat wavering in the air above them. An image of herself running by those goats spun behind Kat's eyes, shifting fast to one of her dragging herself through the heat-baked scrub toward an abandoned oasis. Man, it looked killer hot out there. She drained the last few drops from her water bottle and, licking her dry lips, sank back against the sticky vinyl seat. Talk about exploding and melting!

A few houses were scattered in the distance, all of them same. Square lumps of whitewashed clay with bright blue shutters nestled behind shrubby trees, spiky plants, and low stone walls. These were the bone-dry oases in her imaginary desert, except for the trees. They weren't palm trees. No. These had tiny silvery leaves and were stumpy and twisted, many of them bent over like an old person clutching a cane.

James bounced on the seat. "Whoa, this place is a desert." He batted at Mom's shoulder, then, as if he'd read Kat's mind again, asked, "What kind of trees are those anyway?"

Mom laughed. "Olive."

"Cool," he said, as though she'd told him they were ice cream trees. He bumped Kat's arm with his elbow. "Isn't this cool?"

"Cool? It's about a thousand degrees out there."

"Har, har," said James, wiggling his eyebrows at Kat before shifting his gaze back to the window. "Man," he continued, more to himself, "I've gotta get a postcard of this place."

They drove around the top of the mountain and began to descend. Uncle Nick, their driver, pulled over to stop on the side of the road. "*Koíta*," he said, pointing ahead, "eh, look there. Is, eh . . . Paralia."

His English dribbled out, pretty much like every Greek Kat had heard speaking English since arriving in Greece: slow and thick as if coated with oil, that short *eh* at every hesitation breathy and drawn out.

Mom twisted around. "Look, kids. We're almost there."

James leaned forward and, tugged by what felt like an invisible magnet, Kat did, too. Her stomach squeezed tight. The road dropped off, switching back and forth, the ground on both sides sweeping down and away covered with the same dry scrub of bushes and rocks. Way below, the sea glittered blue and bright as the shutters on the houses.

"Whoa!" James wriggled on his seat. "Check it out! The water's crazy blue."

Mom said something to Uncle Nick, and he chuckled.

"It's called Aegean blue," Mom said to James, her tone teachery and proud. "Greece is the only place the water gets to be that color."

"Coolio! Hey, is that the harbor?" James pointed to where the coast curved away from a small grouping of buildings. "Are those the fishing boats?"

"*Naí, naí,*" said Uncle Nick, nodding, his smile bright under the bristle of his moustache. "*Várka, eínai.*"

"*Várka?* Is that Greek for 'boat'? Sounds kinda like *fart*, right, Kat?"

Kat couldn't take her eyes away from the water. "I—I don't remember it being this blue." The words whispered out of her mouth. And then in a dizzying rush, she did remember. Little girl toes at water's edge, slipping over smooth pebbles before wading into that blue. Aegean or whatever, it was like no other color of the sea: an impossible blue, deep and rich. A blue that had nothing to do with the heat and white and dust she'd been positive waited for her in Paralia.

They drove into the village, and both Kat and James sat tall, craning their heads. On the mountain side of the road was a market, tiered shelves holding baskets full of produce flanking its entrance. Above the shelves hung a rainbow mix of inflated beach balls, towels striped the blue and white of the Greek flag, wide-brimmed straw hats, and tasseled cloth bags. Next to the market was another building, beige and businessy, and next to that one was a building all but hidden behind a long, covered patio full of tables and chairs.

Kat couldn't read the sign nailed to the gate of the covered patio, but a painted picture of a dancing man holding a tray with a wine bottle on it told the tale. *Tavérna*. She'd read about these Greek nightspots in the in-flight magazine. Now she imagined the place at night, full of people and music. Would she be allowed to go? She frowned. The whole of Paralia was pretty much a cheesy little market and a *tavérna*—she had *better* be allowed to go. She squinted to see if anyone sat at any of the tables. *Hmm*. Middle of the day, and all were empty.

"Check out the boats!" James grabbed her arm, pinching her in his excitement. He pointed out his window.

While James chattered on about the boats, Kat took in the harbor, which was no more than a bend in the road that turned into wide, blistered planks of docking that ran out to a squat stone wall with a tall flagpole sticking out of it. Her gaze traveled from the Greek flag flying from the flagpole to the few colorful boats draped with nets bobbing alongside the docks. Beyond the docks and across a small bay was a long line of large rocks jutting into the water to form a jetty. No fishermen were in sight.

"Where is everybody?" said James.

"*Siesta* time," Mom said.

"Wait," said James, "is that the same as in Spanish?"

"Exactly. Greeks take a *siesta* during the hot part of the day."

"Even grown-ups?" said James.

"*Especially* grown-ups." Mom twisted to face them. "I meant to talk to you two about that. The cottage is very small, and you are going to have to be quiet during *siesta*. Yiayiá needs that rest time."

"Don't worry," James said. "We'll go to the beach."

"Ah, *no*." Mom shook her head. "People—especially kids—don't go out during *siesta*. Everything closes down."

"You mean the whole village takes a nap?" Kat didn't even try to hide the smirk in her voice. "She's got to be kidding, right, James?"

He snickered, too.

"No, I'm not kidding. It's too hot to do anything between about noon and three, except lie low. Hey, you don't have to sleep if you don't want, but you may surprise yourself with how tired the heat makes you. Regardless, it's customary to stay home and be quiet during those hours."

For a moment their eyes locked, Mom's gaze pressing into Kat pointy as tacks pushing into a cork bulletin board.

CHAPTER FOUR

bout a mile past the village Uncle Nick swung a left, and the car climbed a dirt road that led up, up, past first one, then another, shorter, narrower lanes. Down each one, cottages lined up in rows facing the sea. Uncle Nick turned left onto the final lane, drove almost to the end, and stopped in front of a dusty wooden gate snugged under an archway woven through with creeping vines.

In a flurry of motion and squeaking vinyl, Uncle Nick, Mom, and James shoved open their doors and slid out of the car. Kat didn't move. Flying all night, then sitting in Uncle Nick's car since late morning had been as hazy as a dream. A dream she hoped she'd wake from. She pulled up her legs, wrapped her arms around her shins, and put her face against her knees. The second she got out of the car, it would all be real. She'd be in Paralia. For the summer. The *whole* summer.

Her door swung open with a loud metallic *clunk*. Startled, she lifted her head as heat and bright and a burst of delighted laughter enveloped her.

"Katina *mou!*" A face poked in, old and female, haloed by dark gray, wiry hair, and wearing a pair of black, heavy-framed glasses.

The woman chortled again, her strong brown fingers stroking Kat's arm. "Do you know who I am?" The words came out in slow, halting dollops—"*Dyu no hchwoo ai em?*"

Kat could only stare at the face: sort of familiar from the latest batch of pictures Mom had tried to show her, but at the same time, not. Too big, too real; a mixture of blinking owl and mischievous elf. Before Kat knew what was happening, the strong fingers drew her from the car and wrapped her in a hug tight enough to make her chest ache. Her nose filled with a deep, rich smell, a blend of sweet soil and melted dark chocolate. The memory came fast. *Geraniums.* She had smelled them close only once before, and only on one person.

"Yiayiá Sofia?"

"*Naí, naí.*" Yiayiá Sofia nodded and drew away, looking up into Kat's face with eyes that swam behind thick lenses.

Yiayiá said more, rubbing her hands up and down Kat's arms. Kat grinned a little, wondering for a second if this was how a puppy felt being petted and *blah-blahed* over.

"*Éla,*" Yiayiá said, leading Kat toward the open gate. "You come."

Inside the yard, dense green bushes bordered the metal fence, creating a small courtyard. Large rust-colored terra-cotta pots filled with geraniums were all around. Smaller pots with more of the flowers stood at each end of wide, worn marble steps leading up to a large stone patio. The flowers were red and pink and white, the blooms so bright that they seemed to float in midair.

Afternoon sun glinted off the front edge of the house, and its gleaming whiteness, broken only by the blue of two closed and shuttered windows, dazzled Kat, making her see spots. She blinked, attempting to focus on the rest of the house, but both it and the reaches of the wraparound patio were almost invisible under the shade of a trellised arbor covered with a nest of vines and leaves. *Were those . . . ? No way.* Hanging here and there through the vines and leaves dangled bunches of purple grapes. Unreal: a scene out of a movie.

Faces and bodies appeared from the depths of the patio. They swarmed, speaking Greek a mile a minute, petting Kat's hair, her arms, her shoulders. Making the *ftou ftou* spitting sound that Kat instantly remembered was the Greek way of adoring the beloved and keeping away the evil. She backed away, almost tripping over a geranium pot, but Yiayiá pulled her forward, holding her at the center of the mass of hugging arms and animated Greek.

"*Yassou, Katina mou!*"

"*Eínai megáli! Eínai oraía!*"

Ftou ftou. And again, *ftou ftou.*

Kat gazed around as if she'd slipped off a path and found herself ringed by strange trees. On one side of her stood a woman about Mom's age. She was stuffed sausage-tight into a sleeveless top and capri pants, her short, dark hair brushed into a shiny pouf that looked as lacquered as wood. On Kat's other side hunched an ancient woman wearing a kerchief that came halfway down her forehead. Her skin was wrinkled to the point of swallowing most of her features, but her fingers held Kat's hands in a firm, almost painful grip, while her smiling mouth spoke in a steady and loud stream.

Behind these two stood two more people. One of them was their driver, Uncle Nick. He talked to a small, slender girl who looked maybe eleven, twelve tops. Kat couldn't honestly tell since the girl faced mostly away. *Jeez, who were all these* people? Maybe she *should've* looked more closely at Mom's photos.

Mom came to her side, and Kat leaned against her shoulder, whispering, "Who are these people? What are they saying?"

"That's my cousin Tassia. She's Nick's wife," Mom said, pointing at poufy sausage woman. "And this," she continued, her hand on kerchief lady's arm, "is Kyría Marula, Yiayiá Sofia's neighbor."

"*Yassou*, Katina *mou*! Hello," said Tassia with a broad smile. She turned to the girl standing with Nick. "Yeorgia," she began, reaching to grab the girl's hand and tug her forward. Tassia wasn't speaking English, but Kat recognized the familiar tone of parental insistence.

"This your cousin Yeorgia," Tassia said, her English slow and choppy, but her voice bright with expectation. "She is your age. She is—ach!" She turned to question Yeorgia, who stood at her side, eyes downcast.

"Twelve," answered Yeorgia to the patio floor.

"*Naí*, twelve," said Tassia, nodding as if the word *twelve* made it a done deal. "You are good friends."

"Tassia *mou*," Mom said, clicking her tongue as she shook her head. "Katina is fourteen—*dekatéssera*—not twelve."

Kat wanted to add that she was turning fifteen in less than three months, but Tassia was waving her hand, saying, "Is okay. One year. Two years. Is nothing."

Tassia murmured at Yeorgia now, nudging her almost on top of Kat. Yeorgia took a tiny step back, raising her eyes slow enough that Kat knew she was equally uncomfortable.

"Welcome, Katina," Yeorgia said, each syllable round and heavy. "I hope you like Greece."

"Thanks," said Kat, pasting a smile on her face and inwardly shrugging when Yeorgia dropped her eyes again.

"*Brávo*," said Tassia. She gave Kat's cheek a firm pinch and, taking hold of Yeorgia's arm, marched her up the steps.

Kat twisted to Mom. "What was *that* about?"

"They're helping Yiayiá with the lunch."

"Oh," said Kat. The way she said it had Mom squeezing her shoulder.

"Don't worry, I know it's a lot of new faces, but Nick's family—and by the way, you should call him 'Theíos Nick'—and Kyría Marula's family have cottages on this lane, too, and pretty soon you'll figure out who's who. And almost everyone speaks a little English, except maybe Marula. Besides, to answer your question, all they're saying is that you've gotten big and beautiful. And that you don't look much like me, meaning you must've gotten your blue eyes and blonde hair from your father."

"My hair is so not blonde," said Kat, swiping a hand over her head. But looking at the faces around her, she got how they could see her hair as blonde. Compared to theirs, her light brown hair was a bleach job. Now that she thought about it, everything about her was light compared to these people. Not because they'd all been baking out in the Greek sun either. No, both Theíos Nick and the women had skin that though pale still had an olive cast to it. And their hair was uniformly dark to the point of blackness, their eyes deep and brown as shiny coffee beans. Like Mom's. Like—

Kat's gaze darted from Mom to James. Their profiles, the way their hair waved all over the place—the same. A boy she hadn't noticed at first (probably another cousin) stood next to James. Her eyes went blurry. The two boys faced each other, smiling and gesturing, their hair, noses, teeth, skin identical as mirror images.

Kat swallowed a lump that sliced at the back of her throat.

At home it had never bothered her that she didn't look much like Mom or James. But here? She touched her cheeks, her nose, aware of how covered with freckles they were. Here she felt like a—a mutant from outer space!

Moments later, Yiayiá led Kat up the steps to where the arbor-covered patio wrapped around the side of the house, depositing her at a long table tucked in the shadiest corner. Kat slid behind the table and slumped down on a narrow, wooden bench. She rubbed crust from her too-tired eyes, let her head *thump* back against the house's smooth, hard exterior wall, and stared up into the dappled green and brown of the grape arbor. How was she going to do this? Be here *all* summer when she couldn't even speak the language? She glared at Mom's back, giving her a double dose of her hairy eyeball.

Then Yiayiá was there, pressing a glass of water into Kat's hand. Kat looked away, blushing. From the smile that played around Yiayiá's mouth, Kat had the sense Yiayiá read her thoughts exactly.

Behind Yiayiá, Tassia and Yeorgia came *clackety-clacking* through a curtain made of strung bamboo beads, carrying large platters of food.

Yiayiá gestured to the glass in Kat's hand. "Drink *neró*, eh, water. Then, eat."

Kat forced a smile and put the glass to her mouth. The water tasted deliciously cold, but the liquid burned against the tightening ache in her throat. She didn't want to be here; she wanted to go home. Right this minute, *this second*. Except not to the rented cardboard Shady Hills house. She wanted her old home, on her old road. Her old room. For a single dizzying moment, the wanting was beyond powerful, clawing at her, a physical pain. She took another sip of water, and another, watching as Yiayiá loaded a plate with shiny crescent-shaped fried potatoes and gleaming meatballs, slices of tomato and cucumber, and small squares of feta cheese. Kat's empty stomach twisted, but the thought of putting food in her mouth made her want to gag.

Everyone was at the table now. Mom, sitting across from her, spooning meatballs onto James's plate. Tassia, making an impatient chopping motion with her hand at Theíos Nick before pouring a glass of iced tea. Yo—*all right, this was bad.* When their eyes met, Cousin-Forgotten-Name, looking startled as a mouse, ducked her head and continued eating. Kat stared back down at the yellow and orange swirls covering the vinyl tablecloth. She wrinkled her nose and gave her eyes a quick swipe. She hadn't cried in years—in *forever*—and she wouldn't start now, in front of all these strangers. She was tired, that was all. Really, really tired.

Yiayiá slid a plate in front of her, and the hot-oil smell of fried potatoes and meatballs teased at Kat's nose. She stabbed a meatball with her fork and nibbled at the brown crust. Salty, but the spiced pink meat in the center was unexpectedly too sweet. She tried a small bite of potato next. Better. She took a bigger bite.

Yiayiá dipped a piece of bread into the juice oozing from tomato slices on Kat's plate. "Try," she said, holding it to Kat's mouth. "Is good."

The bread melted on Kat's tongue, tasting like ripe, tomatoey salad dressing.

Yiayiá laughed. "Is good?"

"Yeah," Kat said, offering a ghost of a smile. "I mean, *naí.*"

"Kat?" It was Mom, beaming as if she were about to give

Kat a present. "Marula's grandson is visiting. He's your age, maybe a little older. Marula says he speaks good English. Isn't that great?"

Kat opened her mouth to respond, then noticed that both Marula and Tassia studied her as if she were a piece of fruit they were thinking of buying.

"Wow," she managed. She tried to make herself smile, but her lips stuck to her teeth. "You know what? I'm super, super tired." She slid from behind the table, coming around to Mom. "Um, where am I supposed to sleep?" she said, touching Mom's shoulder.

"*Aiii*." Mom grabbed Kat's hand. "Your hand is ice." She made a comment in Greek, and everyone chuckled and looked at Kat. Her face burning, Kat lowered her eyes to her hand in Mom's. What she wanted to do was shake Mom hard for bringing her here and dumping her in the middle of these gawking strangers. Of course, she did no such thing, because a small bit of her didn't want to do that at all. That bit wanted to cling to Mom, cling to her until the moment came when they would drive back to the Athens airport, get on a plane, and fly home.

CHAPTER FIVE

om steered Kat a few steps away from the table to two
doorways standing kitty-corner, both hung with bamboo
bead curtains. One, Kat knew, led to the kitchen, because
she remembered it was where Yiayiá and the others came out
with the plates of food. Mom went to the other doorway.

"This is you," she said, parting the hanging beads and gesturing for Kat to go through.

The room was tiny and almost completely taken up with a
double bed covered with a bright, loosely knit blanket. Next
to the bed was a small, squat cupboard, a good-sized flashlight
resting on top.

"I know it's small," said Mom, walking to one of two windows and drawing open the curtains. "But I've decided to share
the other spare room with James, so you can have your own
room."

Kat slumped down on the bed, next to where her backpack and suitcase already sat. The mattress sagged as though
the springs were about to give out. She started to say as much
and caught Mom's face—hopeful and happy, as if Mom remembered something good—and held her tongue, instead taking in
the rest of the room.

The walls were painted a cool blue, but the breeze puffing

out the gauzy yellow curtains whispered through the room, hot and dry. Restless, Kat stood, joining Mom at the window.

Through the screen, Kat had a grainy view of the patio. The table full of relatives was so close that if she put her hand out the window she could practically pat James on the head. She turned to the beaded curtain in the doorway, then back to the window. The screen wasn't even attached. She pushed at it, and it moved, scraping the sill.

"Careful," said Mom, "it looks like it might fall out."

Kat pulled her hand away.

"I know it's not exactly private," Mom said with a small laugh, "but I think you'll be very comfortable."

"Yeah . . . right." Kat dropped down on the bed again, fixing her eyes on the floor. She wrapped her braid tight around her fist, chilled by how much she wished she was anywhere but in this tiny room. "First," she murmured, "you tell me, 'Kat, we're going to Paralia for the summer.' Then, it's, 'No point in bringing your laptop or your phone, because not only is there no cell service or Wi-Fi, but there's no electricity.'" She looked up, pinning Mom with a hot stare. "Now, I'm in a room that's about as private as a—a hamster cage. Anything else you want to, I don't know, *share?*"

Mom sat on the bed, and their knees bumped. She put her arm around Kat.

"Come on, sweets. I know this isn't what you wanted to do this summer. But we're here now, so please." She paused, stroking a hand up and down Kat's arm. "It's been a long time since I've been here. Such a long time. I . . . I want you to give being here—being here in Greece with me, with the family—a chance. And I do think you must be tired from the jet lag. See? A *siesta* is a good idea."

A siesta.

Sure, Mom, whatever you say. That's what Kat wanted to say, but she didn't. What was the point?

Silent, unamused laughter burned the back of Kat's throat as she watched Mom clatter out through the beaded, fake door.

There was no point. No point at all.

CHAPTER SIX

Kat woke with a start, her head jerking up from the pillow into absolute dark. For a split second, she didn't know where she was, didn't recognize the hollow *clacking* sound that woke her. As she scrubbed gummy sleep-grit from her eyes, she remembered: *hanging beads, tiny room, Paralia.*

She groaned, rubbed her eyes more, and reached for her watch. She'd set the time the day before—or was it the night? This jet lag was screwing her up. She pressed the glow button. It was 3:47 a.m., Greek time. With another groan, she rolled over, attempting to get comfortable and go back to sleep.

She couldn't. She sat up, plumping the two pillows behind her and looking toward the windows and doorway. Not a speck of light. Plenty of noise, though. The silvery hiss of crickets mixing with the pressing dark made her head feel wrapped in crinkling fuzz.

She fumbled on the bedside table for the flashlight, flicked it on. The bright circle of light bounced loudly across the walls. She checked the time again. 3:56 a.m.

Now what?

Well, she knew "now what." She crossed her legs. She had to pee—badly. To do *that*, she had to go out to the patio, through the other beaded curtain, and then travel to the complete opposite side of the house.

Outside, a *shush* of warm breeze made the darkness large and boundless. She kept moving, making her way through the other doorway, along the narrow hallway, past the rooms where Yiayiá, Mom, and James slept, down two steps to the kitchen, then up two steps to the bathroom. With relief, she closed the door—*yes, the bathroom had an actual door!*—and hooked it to keep it from swinging open.

She balanced the flashlight on the sink and was tempted to turn it off to avoid seeing the bathroom while she peed. Not only was it so small that her knees practically knocked the door when she sat on the toilet, but it didn't smell good. Not dirty exactly: too much like one of those porta-potties. Closed in, as if the plumbing didn't quite work, and the only way to cover that was with the sour-sweet smell of air freshener.

Done and her hand on the pull-chain flusher, she remembered she was supposed to flush only for poop, not for pee. *Nasty.* She closed the lid and gave her hands a quick rinse, then grabbed the flashlight to make her way back to her room.

Flopping down on the bed, she checked her watch. 4:15 a.m.

4:15 a.m. and she was as awake as awake, and alone as alone.

After cinching on her watch, she hauled up her backpack. This was what she had to get her through the next two months: three FastGrlz novels (she got a tiny spark of pleasure thinking of how Mom, the big English teacher, had groaned when she saw Kat pick them off the shelf at Elm Street Books), a box of stationery, a fat blue pen, an ancient portable CD player (man, she missed her phone), a mongo pack of batteries for said CD player (man, she missed electricity), and the five CDs she'd scrounged from the charity shop. She pushed the books, CDs, and the rest into a pile.

Of course, now there was also the *Runner's Journal*, the surprise gift from Dad she found when she opened her suitcase. She lifted it from the bedside table and, opening it, stared again at the photo taped to the inside cover: Dad holding three-month-old Emma. Under the photo Dad had scrawled, "Run fast, Big Sister Kat. We"—then a big red heart—"U!"

Kat ran her fingertip over Dad's face. When Mom and Dad had first split and he moved to New York City, she saw him pretty often. She and James visited him on the weekends or he showed up at school things like concerts or games and, after, maybe took them to her favorite restaurant in downtown New Canaan, Solé. And sitting there with him, laughing over pizza? That felt almost, *almost* like before the split. Then he met and married Shannon, and everything changed. Nothing to be done there. Divorce and stepparents happened to lots of families, lots of kids. *Woo-hoo*, and on they went.

Until Emma.

Kat got a little teary. Why had she tried to get out of the Paralia trip by calling Dad? They hadn't talked for ages, and he'd sounded way tired. Then, when she'd asked about staying with him in the city, he got quiet—too quiet—before he finally said, "Hmm, let me talk to Shannon." He kept talking, but she hadn't been able to listen anymore.

She cringed now, hearing everything in Dad's too-quiet silence again.

Families were weird. Mom and James and Dad were her family, except here she was, a million miles from home surrounded by olive-skinned Greeks who were also supposed to be her family. She was already a big sister to James, but Dad, whether she wanted him to, or not, was back home adding more family so that now she had a little sister, too. And the worst part was that everyone expected her to be warm and fuzzy about it all.

She stroked the picture of the baby and had the sensation of looking in a mirror, only she was the flat image, the one that wasn't actually there.

Stop! She pressed her thumb and forefinger into her eyes and flipped to the back of the journal and the photo of last year's New Canaan High cross-country team.

Mike Doherty.

She cuddled against the pillows, breathing in his name, his face, everything about him. *What was he doing right now at*—her face squinched up with the effort of figuring the time difference—*at 9:30 on a Thursday night? Home watching TV? Hanging with friends?*

She imagined herself on the couch in her own family room. Mike sat next to her, his shoulder and leg pressed tight to hers. Dream Kat turned to Dream Mike. His face was right there. His eyes, deep and blue—*Aegean blue*—looked right into hers. Then he leaned in.

She could see Dream Mike touch his lips to Dream Kat's, but . . . *then what?* She rubbed a finger over her lips, pushing at them. She'd been kissed one time. Kissed like a real kiss, by a boy. Luke Hamilton, last winter at her friend Angie's birthday party. They were playing flashlight tag out in the dark and cold, the whole group racing around the yard like crazy people. She ran behind a tree and found Luke. They huddled next to each other, breathless and cracking up, and then she looked up at him and his face went serious. The next thing she knew, he dipped his head and put his mouth against hers. They stood that way for a second. And that was it: a moment of pressure and then, nothing.

She looked down at Mike's face, frowned. Kissing Mike would be different—*had to be different*—except how would she find out when she was a gazillion miles away from him?

She dragged her braid free from where it stuck inside the collar of her T-shirt. Who was she kidding anyway? Mike Doherty didn't even know she existed, and he was a senior. Why would a senior notice a freshman?

He would if she were the star freshman on the cross-country team.

Except how was she going to *be* the star freshman now? God, running was the only thing she was even half good at— no, no—*was* good at, or at least *could* be good at. After all, it wasn't her imagination that when the whole eighth-grade class had to run the half mile in gym, she'd gotten the fastest time. It was also not her imagination when Coach Beal came over to her after, bubbly with excitement, saying, "Nicely done, Kat. Hey, you ever thought of doing any distance running?" Isn't that why when the high school forms came, she checked off *cross-country*? And how perfect that she could train with the team all summer. Because she didn't want to be just part of the team, she wanted to be an important part. Then, that sweet, electric jolt when she saw Mike's picture on the team's web page, his expression like he was looking right into her eyes. Hadn't that been a sign that she wasn't going to start high school as the big nothing she'd been at Saxe Middle School?

Kat blew out a breath and closed the journal. The light in the room shifted, brightening by the second. She clicked off the flashlight and twisted up onto her knees to the window. The sun wasn't up, but the glow of the coming morning lit everything outside. Over Yiayiá's fence and far away, the sea spread out, gleaming and wide, a rich carpet rolling out a welcome for her alone.

Maybe . . . maybe her running plan could still work.

Heart beating a little faster, she rushed to where her suitcase lay open on the floor and fished out her gear. She would go running now, down by the sea, before anyone woke up. *Perfect!* Thinking about running made her feel closer to Mike, closer to the team, closer to home.

CHAPTER SEVEN

K at opened Yiayiá's front gate, the squeaky hinges making her hurry through, a prisoner making a break for it. *Escape!* She took off down the lane, laughter at her own silliness bubbling in her throat, even as she knew she didn't want to wake the others. Didn't want to risk anyone interfering with her early morning running plan. Besides, look at the morning. The sky, a deep, smoky blue, was tinged a dark orange that made the tops of the trees and the roofs of the houses stand out stark and black as cutouts. Everything below remained hidden by night, shadowy and indistinct. Kind of spooky.

Her legs lifted and pumped as she ran, and for a moment she imagined her feet leaving the ground, saw herself running into the air, up, up into the morning sky. A fizzy breathlessness rose in her chest. *Love the running?* Easy today. She ran faster. It was good—*really, really good*—to be out on her own.

At the end of Yiayiá's lane, she turned down the hill toward the sea. Gleaming and silvery as fish scales, the water drew her. She lengthened her stride, and when she reached the beach road, her feet turned toward Paralia. The drive from there to Yiayiá's had been short. Surely, she could run to the village and back no problem.

Dry air brushed her skin and, except for the gentle lap of surf over the pebbled beach, the only sound was the crunching *pock pock* of her shoes hitting the packed dirt of the road. She looked up at the houses. Few and scattered, they looked dropped from the sky. No activity around them either. Their shutters closed, the buildings asleep.

She ran on, and the edge of the sun peeked over the sea's horizon. Squinting, she wished for sunglasses as the sun continued to rise, fast and sharp and hot. Blistering. She checked her watch. Barely after 5:00 a.m. *Was this normal?*

She licked her lips. They were parched, papery. She'd forgotten to drink water. *So dumb.* Here she was running out in the middle of nowhere, and she'd spaced on the most important part of being ready to run. She swallowed, trying to get some moisture into her mouth, down her throat. Her calves and ankles stiffened and, with an inward groan, she slowed. She hadn't remembered to stretch either.

Even as her brain told her to stop, turn around, she didn't. Then she saw the narrow blue road sign. Of course, it was in Greek, the letters that funny combination of circles, squiggles, and triangles. Underneath, familiar letters spelled out *Paralia* and *2 kilometers*. That was only a bit more than a mile, making the run to the village and back about two miles. She could do that. At home she'd worked her way up to a mile and a half; two miles should be nothing, right? She slogged on, determined. She *would* run that far, because . . . because she didn't want to go back.

Tendrils of hair stuck to Kat's forehead and neck. The weightlessness of a few moments before disappeared as her legs went heavy and sluggish. Her breathing came in gasps, each lungful of air less satisfying than the one before. Without stopping, she peeled off her tank top and tucked it into the back of her shorts. She'd never run in only her sports bra, but she had to get away from the heat. Pressing on, she chanted to herself, "Around the bend. Paralia is just around the bend."

The sky grew lighter, making everything more distinct, and with the light the bend in the road appeared farther away. She kept her eyes on the sea, willing herself to block out her discomfort by watching the color of the water shift from the shadowy shimmer of the early morning to the iridescent blue of the day before.

Aegean, A-a-a-a-gee-an. She sang the color with every breath, hoping she would at last slip into that running place where her mind forgot her body's effort. If only she had her music! Sighing, she tried visualizing herself racing with the New Canaan team, but instead James popped into her head. Weeks ago, when she started the whole running thing, he'd asked her what it was about. A hint of amusement choked in with her labored breathing. No way would she tell him about Mike Doherty or her cross-country team-queen fantasies. Still, she'd found herself wanting to share a tiny bit of it with him.

"You run and run, and it's like totally killing you. Then you go through this wall? And your body kind of forgets what you're doing and you just run."

"You mean you turn into a robot?" *That James.*

"Yeah, sort of. So even when my head goes, 'Stop,' my legs keep going and going. Sometimes at the end, I'm not even tired anymore and I can run faster."

The way James had looked at her then, as if her skin had

turned to chrome right before his eyes, pushed her to keep running now.

"Love the running," she muttered under her breath, "love it."

At last, she reached the place in the road where the crescent of beach curved toward a short jetty made up of large piled boulders. Then she saw beyond the boulders to the harbor, to the boats, every one of them teeming with life. Bodies twisting and bending and yelling. Acres of yellow net *swish-swishing* over boat railings. Coolers *chunking* as they hit the decks. Engines muttering and gurgling. When Kat neared the docks, without even realizing it, she stopped.

Whoa, fishermen central!

Heads turned, eyes scanning her as if she'd called out her thoughts. At one of the closer docks, an ancient fisherman, his skin nut brown against the white of his shirt, gave her a long, unsmiling once-over. Then he turned away to toss a bundle to the hands reaching toward him from the depths of a large boat.

Heat, and not from running, rose up Kat's neck. *Why did he look at her that way?* Hadn't he ever seen a sweaty girl before? She tugged at the bottoms of her shorts, wishing she'd left on her running tank. *Maybe Greek girls didn't run at dawn. Maybe they didn't even run.*

Her body urged her to run away, back to Yiayiá's. *Don't be crazy.* She twisted and ran deeper into the village, and the clamor of the docks, the fishermen, faded behind her.

Weird. She'd been . . . kind of afraid. Not of the men exactly, but of how they'd stared at her: too fascinated, too curious. What was with that one old fisherman guy, too? She yanked her tank top from the back of her shorts and pulled it over her head. He'd inspected her as if—as if she really *were* a mutant alien from outer space.

When Kat reached the far end of the village, she stopped. Hands on hips, she stood panting on the side of the road. She checked her watch. 5:22 a.m. Including the stop at the docks, the run had taken her a total of about twenty minutes. Twenty minutes that, in this thick, swimming heat, had dragged like hours. Sweat dripped into her eyes, making them sting as she wiped them. She'd been in Paralia for less than twenty-four hours, and it already felt like she'd been away from home for a lifetime.

A cramp of pressure rose from her belly to her chest. Forget Paralia, how was she going to run in this idiot heat? She walked a little half circle, forcing herself to take slow, easy breaths, then walked over to a large rock by the side of the road. She put her palms against the gritty surface and pushed her legs out behind to stretch her calves.

She had to figure out the running thing. Because if she couldn't run—the photo of Mike and the cross-country team spun in her brain. *No.* She needed to focus on her running tips, the ones for running in heat, like—like *more* water and *more* stretching. *Yeah.* She'd drink gallons of water, stretch until her body was a rubber band, because no way was she giving up the running. *No. Way.*

Circling her shoulders now, Kat stood tall, bending her knee so she could grab her ankle for a thigh stretch. The mountain road went up and up, winding one way and then the other in long snaking curves. Through the haze of heat, she made out the top. There was the place where Theíos Nick stopped the car. It looked pretty far, but not *that* far.

That was it! Maybe spending the summer in Greece meant she couldn't train with the New Canaan team right now, but there was a way she could turn herself into the running-goddess-of-life. Hill training. By the time she got back to New Canaan, she'd have trained harder than anyone on the team. Because by the end of the summer, she was going to be able to run to the top of this mountain.

CHAPTER EIGHT

K at trudged back through Paralia. What she wanted was a big glass of—she frowned. What did Yiayiá call water? *"Neró,"* she said, her voice ringing so loud in the quiet that she looked around fast to make sure she was alone. She was, but, with a flicker, lights came on ahead in the market.

Maybe she should go in, see what kind of shopping Paralia offered. *Nah.* She was totally sweaty and didn't have any money. *Lame.* The real reason was that it'd be uncomfortable. Weird even. Because whoever was inside would talk to her in Greek, and what would *she* do?

With a tinkle of bells, the market door opened and a youngish woman holding a basket of peaches came out.

The woman smiled at Kat, calling, *"Kaliméra."*

Kat froze. Why . . . she'd understood. Maybe not the exact words, but the tone. The woman was saying a kind of *hi.* Kat smiled back a tiny smile, and said, *"Ka-li-mé-ra."*

The woman's face brightened. While she unloaded peaches from the basket, she spoke more, then paused, regarding Kat. Kat shrugged, sort of smiled. *So much for understanding.*

"American?"

"Naí." Kat nodded.

"You speak *elliniká?"*

Kat shook her head, and the woman let out a friendly chuckle. "Is okay. I speak English"—she pinched her fingers—"a little." She laughed again and, with a bright "Antío" for Kat, picked up the now-empty basket and went back into the store.

Her mood lighter, Kat wandered toward the harbor. All the boats were gone except the one closest to the road, the one belonging to the old, staring fisherman guy. As she came around to the beach side of the jetty, she studied the sea. Way in the distance, a couple of tiny dark dots moved on the water. What would it be like to be out there, on a fishing boat all day?

A splash caught the corner of her eye.

In a rush of rising water, a shape surfaced. She registered the head and chest of a boy, then . . . everything fell away. Breath stolen, she stood pinned by a thousand darts of hot. He was— Kat's brain couldn't conjure a clear thought of what he was.

The boy shook his head, and droplets of water flew from his hair. Rubbing more water from his eyes, he moved toward the beach. The second his eyes found her, Kat jolted, as if he'd reached out a hand and touched her. But not her skin. A place inside. Dazzled, she had to look away, down. He was far enough off that she couldn't make out the specifics of his eyes, his nose, his mouth, but she knew he was the most beautiful boy she'd ever seen. The knowledge overwhelmed her, making her simultaneously want to wade into the water and run as far from him as she could get.

She didn't move, couldn't. Her eyes traveled back. The boy hadn't moved either. For a second, she was surprised he was still there. That he was real, instead of a fantasy cooked up in her overheated brain. He was so—*wow*. The way his wet hair glistened, tangling against his head and neck. The smooth light brown of his shoulders, chest, belly—

Her whole head went hot, jerking up. *Was he?* No, he couldn't be. *Naked* barely entered her consciousness when his eyes caught hers again. His knowing amusement buzzed at her, even before one side of his mouth curled up. Her lips twitched, a smile beginning. Then a voice as tired and crusty as the bark of an old dog called out.

"Theofilus!"

The boy turned, and Kat looked, too. The old fisherman she'd seen earlier on the docks stood there again, his large fishing boat looming behind him. He raised an arm, beckoning.

"Theofilus. *Éla!*"

The boy waved to the man and, after tossing her a brilliant smile, dove back under the water.

Long, easy strokes took him to the docks, and when he lifted himself onto the planking, she took in the wet cling of his low-slung khaki shorts. *Of course, he wasn't naked.* Why had it even occurred to her that anyone would be swimming naked in broad daylight, right in the center of a village? *The heat.* She was a whack job, a jet-lagged heat victim.

Not true, a secret inner voice whispered. For a single beat his nakedness had meant something . . . more. Something beyond. As if he'd appeared from nowhere. A magical being emerging from the sea. For her and only her.

Her face went hot again. *Stop. Staring.* Her eyes stayed on him, though. Stayed as he slid on a loose white shirt and without buttoning it followed the older man. Stayed as he hopped onto the side of the fishing boat and stood tall, his shirt billowing out and his hair lifting away from his face, as the boat headed out to sea.

CHAPTER NINE

heofilus. That had to be his name. Kat walked along the beach toward Yiayiá's and, even as some faraway part of her listened to her running shoes *crunch-crunching* into the pebbles, felt her sweaty clothes stiffening against her skin, she didn't care. *Theofilus.* She liked how the first sound caught her tongue between her teeth, how the syllables stretched as they rose and fell.

She faced the water, shading her eyes. Way out chugged the long flat gray of a distant tanker, but she could no longer see any of the fishing boats. He was out there, though. Out there, fishing in all that impossible blue.

Mike's picture flared behind her eyes and she shook her head, heaving out a loud breath. *Totally pathetic.* Was this her fate? To get googly over guys she didn't know? Guys she had no chance of ever even meeting?

Dropping down onto the beach, she plunged her hands into the pebbles. The top layer of stones was warm and smooth, but underneath waited the gritty, wet coolness of the sea. The smell of salt and seaweed drifted into her nose as she raked her hands in again and again, and bits of stone dug under her nails to the prickly point of hurting. That was what thinking of that boy Theofilus was like: a shivery kind of almost pain. *Like running.* She raked her fingers deeper. Like pushing herself on a run until the pain of it mixing with the need to keep going gave her a momentary and bizarre kind of bliss.

She glanced at her watch. Almost 6:15 a.m. For sure Mom, and probably everyone else, was awake by now. Cursing herself for not leaving a note, she headed away from the water.

On the road, the sun's glare on the chalky surface blinded her. She blew out a long breath and set off, head low and seeing a pair of huge, dark sunglasses in her future.

A ways ahead, an engine sputter became a fast-moving whine coming toward her. She looked up and spotted a motorbike in the distance. As it got closer, she gritted her teeth against the grating racket, glancing up only when it was almost on top of her.

Thin and battered, it was a motorbike in the true sense of the word *bike*, looking almost identical to the one James rode around on at home, except with a motor attached to the frame. A dark-helmeted man wearing long pants and a long-sleeved shirt rode the bike. As he buzzed by, Kat fixed her eyes on her feet and kept walking.

With a coughing snarl, the bike slowed and revved, changing direction. She stiffened, expecting to feel the whizzing rush of air when the bike raced past her again. It didn't race by.

And didn't race by.

She glanced over her shoulder. The biker crept along a couple of car lengths behind.

The pulse in her neck began to bump. Between the shiny black void of the helmet's closed visor and the sputtering pant of the engine, it was as though a hulk-headed animal had chosen to follow her home.

She took her time turning her head forward but crossed

her arms over her chest and walked a bit faster. What was this guy's problem? Anxious giggles bubbled in her throat. *Maybe she should ask him.*

Scanning the landscape ahead, Kat hoped to see buses and cars filling the road. Nope, nothing. No one but her, still a long walk from the turnoff to Yiayiá's lane, and her shadow, Helmet-Man.

He was probably a tourist, too. Taking in the view. Or maybe he wanted to offer her a ride, but was shy and—*What did he want? Why didn't he come up beside her? Talk to her, jeer at her, pinch her butt, something?*

The motorbike revved and, as if she'd been hit by a shot of electricity, Kat veered off the road onto the beach, ears roaring, brain gasping. *Don't look. Don't even look.*

Dashing to the water's edge, she kicked off her shoes. She was just going for a swim. *Right.* She hurried into the sea, taking long, reaching strides, until at last she could dive under a wave.

She swam deeper and deeper, fierce satisfaction feeding every stroke. She would stay underwater until Helmet-Man got bored with his stupid little game and disappeared, hopefully off the face of the earth.

CHAPTER TEN

Dripping with salt water and fuming, Kat stomped down Yiayiá's lane. *Stupid, stupid Helmet-Jerk!* Of course, she was glad he was gone when she came up for air, but still. Because of his idiot game, not only was she later than ever, but also she'd ditched her shoes too close to the water and now they were soaked.

She put her hand on Yiayiá's gate and paused, expecting to hear Mom and Yiayiá, maybe even James, jabbering frantically about what had happened to her and where could she be.

All was hushed, except for a muted spattering. She pushed through the gate, freezing when she spotted Yiayiá's broad back rocking side to side in a far corner of the yard. The spattering came from the spray of the hose hitting pots as she watered her flowers. Kat scanned up to the patio. Empty. Maybe she could avoid anyone knowing she'd been gone at all. She would dash—

Yiayiá turned and gave a start, blinking once, twice at Kat. She twisted the hose's nozzle, turning off the water. "*Ti káneis, vre* Katina?" she said, looking Kat up and down.

What was she doing? Kat offered up her blank, confused smile, and shrugged. "*Kaliméra?*"

"*Kaliméra?*" Yiayiá put her free hand on her hip and, waving the nozzle, sprayed Kat not with water but with a steady rain of hot Greek.

Kat didn't move. Wackily enough, being scolded in a foreign language was not bad. Kat fought to keep from smiling, imagining she was one of Yiayiá's flower pots getting dumped on. Then Mom came out onto the patio.

"What is going on out here?" she said to Kat, before turning to Yiayiá. "Mamá?"

Rat-a-tat-tat, went Yiayiá at Mom, and then *doh-di-doh-di-doh*, explained Mom to Yiayiá. The good part was that even though they sounded like they were arguing, no one argued with Kat. The bad part was that standing there in the yard in her wet, salty running clothes *and shoes* was becoming a drag.

Kat shifted from squishy foot to squishy foot. Plucked at her soaking tank top. A shower would be good right now. A nice, long, cool shower. She closed her eyes, picturing their shower at home, then heard Mom say, "Olympics." Kat's eyes snapped open. *That's* how Mom was explaining her running to Yiayiá? Before she could think to stop herself, she burst out laughing.

Both Yiayiá and Mom turned to stare at her. "What's so funny?" said Mom.

Yiayiá spoke, too, and from the mirror tone of her Greek, Kat knew she asked the same question.

"Nothing, I . . . I was wondering where the shower was."

"*Ti léei?*" said Yiayiá.

Mom said a couple of words out of the side of her mouth to Yiayiá. Yiayiá nodded and cranked her sprayer back on, aiming it first at Kat and then at Mom. Shrieking and giggling, both Kat and Mom scrambled up the steps.

"That is one crazy lady," said Kat, breathless now.

"Yes, just another crazy Greek," said Mom. Her chuckle stretched into a yawn. "I need coffee. Strong Greek coffee." She rubbed her fingers over her mouth, then stopped her hand, looking Kat up and down the way Yiayiá had. "How long have *you* been up?"

"A while," Kat murmured, edging back toward her room. She had no interest in telling Mom about her morning or getting caught in a lie.

"I can't believe you went running already," Mom said, moving with her. "How was it?"

"Hot," said Kat. *That* wasn't a lie. "Really, really hot."

"I can't even imagine. Where did you go?"

"I went . . . to the beach." Kat ran her hand down over the wet tail of her braid, then dropped her fingers, hoping Mom hadn't noticed that she was already drenched before Yiayiá did her spray routine. "Can I take a shower?"

"Oh, of course," said Mom, but she didn't move, just kept scrutinizing Kat.

Here we go. Kat made her eyes big. "What?"

"It's only that Yiayiá was worried. Now, don't get mad," she whispered, as if they were up to no good together. "Yiayiá doesn't know anything about cross-country or running. In her eyes, young girls should not be wandering around alone, especially not dressed like that."

"What?" Kat huffed out a breath. "I was not 'wandering around.' And these are running clothes because I was out for a run, you know, exercising?"

"I know. I know. But things are different here and—"

"Running is running, Mom. It's a good thing. Now, will you please tell me where the shower is?"

"I know running is a good thing." Mom's voice trailed off as she glanced back to where Yiayiá tended her flowers. "Okay, okay. The shower. It's around this way."

For a moment there was blissfully no more conversation.

Then Mom spoke over her shoulder, "Did you see anyone down on the beach?"

For a second, Kat wanted to tell Mom about Helmet-Man, but then Mom would probably start in on the "wandering around alone" thing again.

She didn't have to decide, because Mom went around another corner of the cottage. When Kat caught up, Mom's expression had gone anxious and hopeful. Kat frowned when she saw what was behind Mom.

"You are so kidding me." Kat gawked at the makeshift outdoor shower contraption.

Mom sighed. "I am so not."

CHAPTER ELEVEN

"**M**om?" Kat dragged the thin, white plastic curtain aside. "This roughing-it stuff? It's getting stupid now."

"Look. It's not that bad." Mom waved a hand at the patched-together sheets of foggy blue plastic making up the shower's walls. "It's totally enclosed. No one can see you and it's better than the hose."

"Ha, ha," said Kat. She pointed to the large, mottled gray, corrugated metal box that made a kind of half ceiling. "Is that supposed to be where the water is?"

"Mm-hmm. Why don't you get started and I'll find you a towel." Mom turned to go. "And make it short. Clean water is scarce around these parts, because the water truck only comes about once a week."

"What about Yiayiá watering her flowers?"

"Thanks for reminding me," Mom sang over her shoulder. "That's another reason you need to keep your shower short. Yiayiá needs lots of water for her flowers."

"Ha, again," Kat called at Mom's back.

Biting her lip, Kat stepped into the shower. Light and shadow bled through the clouded walls. She yanked the thin curtain closed and peeled off her running clothes. *No privacy whatsoever.*

Thick as the Paralia heat was, standing there naked made her shiver. She crossed an arm over her chest and turned on the water. The sprinkle was weak but pleasantly warm. She picked up the lone bottle sitting in a corner: Greek scrawled across the label. She flipped off the cap, sniffed. Peppermint. *Well, it better be soap.* She slathered it over her body and into her hair.

Hmm, and hmm again. Hands swabbing her face, Kat enjoyed the slippery softness of her skin when the sweaty-salty crust from her run, and subsequent dive into the sea, washed away. Glancing up, she had the sensation that the open sky had come closer, the warm weight of it keeping her company in the shower. This was not bad. A tightness inside her chest unraveled. Not bad at all.

As she tipped her face back into the shower, a faint buzz whined—motorized and familiar.

Helmet-Man!

She jerked her head from the spray, straining her ears. *Pat-a-pat* went the shower, and from the other side of the house, the indistinct rise and fall of voices. She was sure she heard a motorbike, but *so?* She'd seen dozens of them since landing in Greece. Was she now going to freak every time she thought she heard an idiot motorbike?

She reached to turn off the water but jumped back, covering herself with her hands when the curtain slapped open. Gnarled fingers poked in, turning off the water with a quick crank. Then Yiayiá's head appeared.

"Water," she said, pointing up to the spout. "Too much."

Yiayiá held out a towel, continuing to talk in Greek as if they were sitting at the breakfast table. Kat grabbed the towel, fumbling as she draped it over herself.

The ringing metal of a chain-link gate crashing open, followed by high-pitched laughter and the rush of running feet made Kat grip the towel closer. Yiayiá's head disappeared. "Boys! Quiet!"

Kat stood as though spellbound, listening to the *chop-chop* of voices talking, laughing, talking. Now she could hear the girl cousin's voice, Yo—*what was her name?* Then James, "Hey, is this the shower? Coolio! Oops, sorry, Kat."

Kat stared into his smiling face, watched as it crinkled and smirked before ducking out. *That did it.* Holding her towel around her as best she could, she marched out of the shower. James, Yiayiá, clone-boy Cousin Nikos, and Cousin Yo-*whatever* were right there. They stopped talking to stare at her. She took a breath, then another. Maybe her whole body would simply go up in flames. Now, Mom came around the corner.

"This is—unbelievable!" Kat snapped. "It's like a spanking bus station around here!"

She stalked by the group, her fury reaching new heights when sputters of amusement from both boys erupted behind her.

She was about to shove through the curtain to her room when Cousin Yo called.

"Katina?"

Kat whipped around.

Eyes baby deer-wide, Yo-Yo held out her soggy pile of running gear. "You forget this, eh, at the shower."

"Oh, yeah. Thanks." Kat's anger deflated. She reached for her gear and almost lost her towel. "I'm sorry. What was your name again?"

"Yeorgia."

Your-YEE-uh. "Right. Do you mind bringing my things in here, Yeorgia?"

Yeorgia followed Kat, but stopped when she went to put the running gear on the bed.

"This is very wet," she said. "You wear this. For swimming?"

Kat looked up from rummaging through her suitcase. "No, I tried to go for a run." She puffed out a dismissive little breath. "Forget it. Drop everything on the floor, okay?"

"What is . . . *run?*"

"You know," said Kat, throwing a fresh bathing suit on the bed. "Running?" She made a running motion and had to make another quick grab to keep on her towel. "Sports? The Olympics?"

"*Naí, naí,*" said Yeorgia, gazing at her as if she were a pop star. Then her face went bright red. "*Sygnómi.* I'm sorry, Katina. You want to dress now. I—my mother is waiting. I go." Yeorgia backed toward the doorway.

Yeorgia's discomfort had Kat gripping her towel tighter. "Sure. I'll see you later. Thanks for the help, and . . . about before . . . I didn't mean to blow up like that."

"Is okay." Yeorgia smiled quick and wide. "We have this shower also. I don't like. Nikos, eh, he is throwing things." She mimed tossing, then shook her head, the weight of the world resting on her shoulders. "Understand?"

Huh. The universal language of little brothers. "Yes." Kat let out a short laugh. "I totally understand."

CHAPTER TWELVE

Later that morning, Kat hunkered down under the awning of Yiayiá's patio swing, a book propped on her thighs. She'd never admit this to Mom, but the first FastGrlz book sucked wind; too full of girl characters who either had slick, fast answers for every situation or did the stupidest stuff on the planet. *And yippee—she had two more!*

At the end of a chapter, she flung the book aside. It slid across the slippery vinyl of the swing's seat cushion and thumped to the floor. She didn't pick it up. Between the morning's growing heat and her dull, jet-lagged frame of mind, moving took too much effort.

Through slitted eyes, she observed Mom and Yiayiá. They sat across the patio, near each other, but each in her own world: Mom reading a book and Yiayiá doing some kind of knitting project that used only one needle. Kat studied Mom. *Hmm.* Long way to travel to sit there reading a book.

Boy laughter burst from the yard below. James and Nikos. They were attempting to inflate a large yellow raft with a bicycle pump. Wearing nothing but brightly colored baggy surf shorts and T-shirts wrapped around their heads sheik-style, they looked more like clones than ever.

Their resemblance was not just about their looks, either: it was their expressions, the way they thought, what they did. Like now. Nikos pumped the bicycle pump so furiously that it tooted. Poking Nikos hard, James tucked his hand under his own armpit and flapped his elbow like a chicken wing, making a similarly airy farting noise. Nikos dropped the pump, imitating James until both boys cracked up.

"Hey," Kat called down, "that raft doesn't look like it's holding air."

"It's full of holes," said James. "We're figuring out where to patch it."

Nikos said a couple of words to James, then James snickered, nodding his head, saying, "*Naí, naí.*"

Both boys headed for the steps. As they climbed, Nikos whispered to James. "Eh, Dimitri," was all Kat could make out. She frowned as they strolled over.

"Who's Dimitri?" said Kat.

James's face broke into a blinding grin. "Me. It's a name a lot of Greeks use for James. Cool, huh?"

Nikos elbowed him, and James's smile grew. "Oh, yeah. So, Kat, do you want some *skatá malakós?*"

Kat's frown deepened. Not only was she sure the boys were up to no good, but it also ticked her off that James—*excuse me, Dimitri*—was picking up the whole Greek thing incredibly fast. It was as if, along with his skin and hair and eyes, his tongue brimmed with Greek genes ready to spout off in the mother tongue.

"What's that? Some bizarro Greek coffee drink?"

Both boys exploded with gurgling sputters of laughter.

"What?" she said, then clamped her lips tight. "You know what? I don't even care."

Bent over in hysterics, James tried to talk. "I told—I told

Nikos you'd think it was a coffee thing. No wait. Don't get mad. You're gonna think this is funny."

"Yeah, right," she said, raising her eyebrows. "Give."

"*Skatá malakós* means soft, you know . . ." James practically shook with delight. He lowered his voice, but shot a quick glance Mom's way to make sure she wasn't listening. "The swear for poop."

"You guys." Kat shook her head but couldn't help cracking up with them. "Go fix your stupid raft so we can go to the beach."

She watched the boys frolic down the steps like two sweaty puppies, and she pulled her *Runner's Journal* onto her lap. She thumbed to a blank page. "*Skatá malakós*," she wrote, then two dashes and "soft, the swear for poop."

She studied the words. Maybe she'd feel less out of place if she could speak the language a bit. She wrote more. *Naí* was "yes," and *óchi* was "no." *Kalós* was "good," and *kakó* was "bad." *Ti* meant "what," and *thélo* was "I want." *Korítsi* was "girl"; *agóri* was "boy." Then slow and secret, she wrote the word that had been in her mind all along.

Theofilus.

She stroked the pen over his name, making each letter fat and thick and blue. Blue like the sea. Where he was right now. She closed her eyes, recapturing that moment when she first saw him, and exhaled long and slow, the place behind her belly button dipping down, loose and warm.

Opening her eyes, she riffled pages until she came to the picture of the cross-country team. *Mike.* She brought the journal close, studying his features, his expression, imagining seeing him live and in person. Would it be the same as when she saw Theofilus?

A loud popping *hiss* startled her. James and Nikos stood over the now-flat raft, their hands planted on their hips.

Kat stared at the raft, then shoved at the floor with her foot until she swung. What was with her? Why did she sit here pumping herself full of a Greek boy she saw swimming for thirty seconds? She shook her head and shook it again as she lifted her sweaty braid off her sweaty neck. Being in Paralia was pushing her to all new levels of deluded lameness.

Running. That's what she needed to be thinking about.

She thumbed to the front of the journal, read,

Day One: 5:30 a.m. Too hot. Helmet-Man, ugh!

She turned the page, tapped her pen against her thigh. So? Running during the heat of the day—*which was the whole day*—wouldn't work. Maybe if she lived here for the rest of her life, she'd get used to it, but at this rate?

In her mind's eye, the bright smiles of the cross-country team taunted her. Before leaving New Canaan, she'd studied the team's summer training schedule. By now, they were probably all running at least three miles a day. She ached for her phone and an internet connection. If she had those, she could at least check the team page. *Gah!* She snapped the journal shut and pressed her head back. Being unplugged in Paralia was like being stuck up to her neck in cement. *Except . . .*

Except for that moment when she saw Theofilus. She bumped her head back. All she knew about him was that he was beautiful and he'd headed out on a fishing boat with that old fisherman who gave her the evil eye. When would they even come back? Before the *siesta*? Later? After dark?

After dark, darkness, alone, Helmet-Man.

Her imagination spun to where the black-helmeted biker

of that morning morphed into dozens of black-helmeted bikers, all racing after her on a dark road.

Forget. About. That!

The biker incident was a freaky twist, and she wouldn't let it make her afraid, or afraid of the dark, because . . . Knowledge spread through her, an injection of ice.

Because that's when she had to go running.

There it was. No choice. If she wanted her running to go anywhere, she had to go before the sun came up, or after it went down.

Only, did she have the nerve to run in the dark? She squeezed her eyes shut tight, her lack of nerve making her stomach flip and flop. Well, she had to *find* some nerve. She had to—her flipping, flopping stomach went hot—to try to find Theofilus.

She sat up with a start as cool paper thudded on her thighs. Her book. Yiayiá had dropped it in her lap and now pointed at it, saying, "*Kaló korítsi?*"

What? Kat looked down at the book, then reddened, her eyes shooting to Yiayiá's face. Wait. Could Yiayiá tell she was having steamy thoughts about a boy? Is that what she meant by "good girl"?

Yiayiá expelled a loud breath that sounded as frustrated as Kat felt and tapped the book again, this time slower, repeating her question.

"You mean her?" Kat pointed to the book cover where a skeletally thin teen girl in a super-tight, super-short dress sat at the center of an assortment of adoring teen boys. "Is *she* a 'good girl'?" Kat had to snicker. "No. Óchi, Yiayiá. She's bad," she said, wiggling her eyebrows, "*kakó.*"

Yiayiá goggled at her, then let out a low, rumbling chuckle, plucking up the book. She waved it high, speaking over her shoulder to Mom. Then they both laughed.

Warmth, unexpected and bright, coursed through Kat. *How about that?* She'd managed to have a whole conversation with Yiayiá. In Greek.

"Hey, Kat!" James called. "You ready to go to the beach?"

"Uh-unh." Kat shook her head and stood, every nerve in her body ready to spring. "I think I'll walk into Paralia."

"Paralia?" said Yiayiá, raising her eyebrows. "Why?"

"I don't know. To, you know, check it out."

"Maria?" Yiayiá called to Mom. "Katina . . ."

Now Yiayiá and Mom were in full discussion mode. Kat chewed her lip, attempting to read their faces. *What was the big deal?* Of course, the reason she wanted to walk into town was to scope around for Theofilus, but they didn't know that.

By the time Yiayiá and Mom stopped talking, Kat thought she would burst.

"Paralia. Okay," said Yiayiá, nodding with a firm smile. "We go. Together."

CHAPTER THIRTEEN

W alking, Kat glanced at Yiayiá. Wearing her wide-brimmed straw hat pulled down to the rims of her glasses and a robe-dress thingy that rippled around her calves like a magician's cape, Yiayiá cruised forward, a human ocean liner. With an inward shrug, Kat tossed her braid over her shoulder. Maybe this was better. What would she have done to find Theofilus on her own? Run around from fishing boat to fishing boat looking for him? Wait on the beach until he popped out of the sea again?

No. A small smile crept across her mouth. Being with Yiayiá gave her trip to town a purpose. Her grandmother needed help with a few errands. If that meant running into Theofilus, that would be a surprise. *And a little bit of mission accomplished.* All she'd have to do then would be figure out how to talk to him without Yiayiá getting suspicious.

"Katina?" Yiayiá spoke without turning or slowing down. "*Ti théleis stin* Paralia?"

Théleis? Right, want. "I don't know," Kat said with a shrug. "Nothing, I mean, *típota*, Yiayiá. I . . ." She pointed to her eyes, then toward the town. "I just want to see what's there."

"Paralia is good," murmured Yiayiá, as if it were a food she planned to cook.

They smiled at each other and walked a bit farther, and even though they didn't talk, the silence didn't make Kat itchy. Being with Yiayiá was solid, warm. The way Yiayiá said her name: *Ka-teenah.* At first, she'd wanted to tell Yiayiá to call her Kat, but it was weird. The sound of her full name here, the way it mixed in with the Greek, didn't bug her the way it did at home.

After a moment, Yiayiá said, "You like shopping?"

"Yeah, *naí.*"

"Good." Yiayiá thrust the strap of her handbag into the crook of her elbow. "We shop for *psári.* For fish."

Fish! Kat let out a startled breath. "Will all the fishermen be there?"

Yiayiá gave her a look, searching and measuring. "Fishermen? What you say?"

Kat yanked the bill of her baseball cap lower. "Nothing, Yiayiá."

"Eh, fish? You say you like?"

Kat nodded as if that quick motion alone would shove any conversation about fishermen away. "Yeah, *naí,* I-I like fish."

"*Brávo.* We buy."

By the time they reached town, Kat was pretty sure she could fry whatever fish they bought on top of her head. Yiayiá, on the other hand, looked as fresh as if she just stepped out of an air-conditioned room.

Kat followed Yiayiá onto the docks. Her eyes raced over each boat. She tried to picture Theofilus's boat as it headed out to sea, but she'd been too busy staring at him, and the sun had been way too bright. Was it brown around the bottom with a white pilot box like the one on her left? Or did it have a Greek flag hanging from the stern like this one to her right? What about a name? *Forget that.* The painted Greek letters across each stern were all equally illegible.

Consumed by noise and color, she gazed around while the thick, smoky smells of salty sea and fish, cigarettes and exhaust filled her nose. In or near each boat, fishermen, most crusty with age, but a few younger than James, called out, pointing to their displays of catch, holding up silvery fish and slithery-looking black eels. Further along, kind of like a fisherman sewing party, a group of men and boys sat on the dock, piles of yellow, cobwebby net spread over their legs, their hands busy with repairs. Theofilus was nowhere in sight. Kat squinted, hunting. *Where was he?*

Yiayiá tugged at her arm. "*Éla*, Katina. Come. Look."

Next to them, a fisherman raised what appeared to be a large, gooey, pinkish-gray starfish. Kat made a gagging noise, and Yiayiá tipped her head back, hooting loud and long.

"*Kalamári.*" Yiayiá grabbed her hand. "Squid. You like?"

"No, *óchi*," Kat said. She smiled as she fake-gagged again, laughing, too.

How different it was, being on the docks now. Sure, a couple of fishermen stared, but mostly they glanced and moved on. She was simply here with her *yiayiá*.

Yiayiá cackled more, delighted, and spoke to the fisherman. He nodded and opened a cooler full of thousands of tiny, gleaming fish.

"*Brávo*," said Yiayiá. She held up three fingers, and the fisherman put a piece of newspaper on a scale and loaded scoopfuls of the tiny fish onto the paper.

When her purchase was complete, Yiayiá beckoned to where Kat lagged behind on the docks. "Katina?"

Kat took one more look around the busy docks. No luck. Resigned, she followed. When she reached Yiayiá, she made as if to walk back to the house, but Yiayiá shook her head, saying, "No home, yet."

Kat let Yiayiá tow her along to town. Outside the market, Yiayiá paused to examine the fruit on the shelves, and Kat's gaze shifted back to the harbor. *Why hadn't he been there?*

A gentle tapping on the side of her head.

"Where you go?" Yiayiá said, her expression full of knowing something was up. She touched Kat's head again. "Where you go here?"

Yiayiá's focus kept Kat from looking away. Should she go ahead and ask Yiayiá if she knew Theofilus? Then she'd have to explain how *she* knew him. *Nope. Not a good plan.*

"What?" Kat said at last. She forced a smile, raising her eyebrows in fake confusion.

Yiayiá's eyes—sharp, brown points—continued to study Kat. "Katina *mou*," she said. "There is something," she drew the words out, "something you want?"

The way Yiayiá looked at her—too curious.

"I-I want . . ." Kat glanced around fast and pointed to the market door where a poster of frosty soda bottles hung. "A drink, yeah," she said, making a drinking motion. "I'm super thirsty."

"A drink?" Yiayiá rocked her head, considering Kat. "Okay," she said, "okay."

Inside, Kat made a beeline for the coolers. She looked from bottle to bottle, all swirled with Greek letters, then peeked back to where Yiayiá stood chatting with the man behind the front counter.

How Yiayiá talked to her sometimes. As if she knew—*No.* Kat yanked open the cooler, reveling for a moment in the icy air. *That was crazy.* They could barely understand each other.

Just as she dragged out a yellow bottle covered with cartoony lemon slices, the young woman she'd run into that morning came through a back doorway.

"Ah, *yassou*," the young woman said. She beamed, putting down the crate of drinks she carried.

"*Yassou*," said Kat, smiling back and holding up the bottle. "This is lemon, right?"

"Lemon, yes. Is soda. You want soda?"

"Yeah."

With a wink, the young woman opened the cooler and started unloading the crate.

Kat watched her. What a relief it was to talk to a person who *did* understand what she said. A person who—Kat gripped the bottle hard. Then, clearing her throat, she said, "Excuse me?"

The young woman stopped her restocking. "Yes?"

"I'm wondering." Kat hesitated. *Please let this be a good idea.* She lowered her voice. "Do you know . . . Theofilus?"

"Theofilus?"

Kat swallowed. "He's a-a fisherman."

"*Kalós.*" The young woman went back to her restocking. "You go to the docks. All the fishermen there."

"I've already been there," said Kat, moving her soda from one hand to the other. "A lot of the other fishermen were there. But I didn't see him."

The young woman clicked her tongue and shook her head. "No *all* the fishermen. Many go far out in the sea." She lifted her arm, waving in the direction of the docks, the sea. "They don't come back yet. You go later. You find him."

"Oh, okay," said Kat, a happy little *zing* sparking. "Later, like—"

"Aaah." The young woman's eyes went wide. "Theofilus *Zafirakis? Naí. Naí,*" she said, light and teasing now. "He get here now. Like you. He is good boy. He help his *pappoús* with fishing. He work very hard. Stay on the boat all the time. He is your age, fifteen, maybe sixteen. He is very handsome. You like him?"

Whoa! Kat could only stare, and all at once, Yiayiá was at her side.

"*Yassou,* Thula." Yiayiá patted the young woman's arm, shifting instantly to the Greek version of the "what's up?" tone.

Horrified, Kat watched Thula's mouth open. *No!*

Kat stepped in front of Yiayiá fast, holding up her bottle, saying, "What? Is this lemon? I didn't want lemon."

She yanked open the cooler, twisting to stare hard into Thula's eyes. *Please, please don't say anything about Theofilus!*

Thula stepped back, wrinkling her forehead at Kat. Then with a knowing click of her tongue, she turned to speak to Yiayiá.

Greek streaming around her, Kat returned the lemon soda to the cooler and grabbed a bottle decorated with limes.

After a few more words, Thula said a bright "*Antío*" and, tossing Kat a mischievous grin, disappeared through the back door.

Between embarrassment that Thula knew of her interest in Theofilus and relief that neither woman said his name, Kat exhaled. Her secret was still safe—at least she hoped it was—and Theofilus would be back later.

Yiayiá exhaled, too, strangely mirroring Kat. "Katina, you want something more?"

The words came out simple and innocent, but Yiayiá's eyes gleamed with amusement, and her smile was the pixie-owl smile from their first encounter.

"No. *Óchi*, Yiayiá. I'm good."

Kat unscrewed the top of her drink and sipped. What was it about Yiayiá? One minute Kat was completely comfortable with her, and the next, Yiayiá asked questions that seemed a lot bigger than the words.

CHAPTER FOURTEEN

The next morning, as soon as breakfast was over, Kat plopped down on the swing—it was quickly becoming her favorite spot. She yawned, but not as deeply as she'd been yawning yesterday afternoon and evening. That jet-lag stuff totally messed a girl up.

Since it was another blistering hot day, she resigned herself to the fact that running during the day was pretty much officially a no-go. She'd considered trying to go the day before after the sun set, maybe even trying to find Theofilus on the docks if she made it as far as the town, but gave up that idea. Running twice in one day? Waaaay too tiring.

After dinner, she'd almost asked Mom if they could maybe borrow Theíos Nick's car and drive into Paralia to check out the *tavérna*, but Mom's loud yawning told her that she wasn't the only one with a jet-lag problem.

Kat lifted her legs now, pointing and flexing her toes. Today would be different. She was ready to tackle whatever she could find in this hot, dusty little berg. First order of business: running. She would go *after* the sun set, but *before* it got too dark. Second item: finding Theofilus.

Maybe she should learn more about the fishermen. Would Theíos Nick know? Maybe she could ask Mom and then Mom could ask—? Okay, she needed to make an action plan. She reached to get her journal from an old bag she'd found the day before. The bag was a large, flat square, tightly woven from what once must have been bright blue wool. Now the blue was faded, but the white wool pattern of a geometric Greek key around the top over a scene of a girl aiming an arrow at a running deer was still clear. Kat had never been much for carrying bags. Still, after she came across it in her bedside cabinet, she went looking for Mom to ask if she could use it for the beach.

Instead of finding Mom, she discovered Yiayiá in the tiny, lemony-fishy-smelling kitchen, elbows deep in what Kat was quickly learning was her favorite activity—cooking.

"*Yassou,* Katina," Yiayiá said, wiping flour-dusted hands on her apron. She straightened her glasses to see what Kat had. "Aah, *tagári.*"

"What's *tagári?*"

"Is means, eh, like 'old ways.' Eh, shepherds use." Yiayiá made a jaunty motion as if draping the long strap of the bag over her shoulder and patted the place on her hip where the pouch would rest. "To carry food."

"Right." Kat nodded, then nodded again, almost able to see the language barrier filling the room.

After a moment, Yiayiá said, "This bag, I give your mother. Long time." She gestured to the bag, then to Kat. "You want? To keep?"

Kat started to shake her head but found herself saying, "Sure."

"*Brávo.* Is very Greek. Girls today"—Yiayiá's lips pursed—"want new things. Like new things. Many old things better."

Kat waited, thinking Yiayiá would tell her more, but Yiayiá

dropped her eyes back to the table and continued flouring the tiny fish they'd brought home from the docks.

O-kay, then. Kat was about to duck out when Yiayiá did go on, her voice quiet, arguing with herself. "Artemis is hunter. Like your *mamá.*" She chopped her palm at the *tagári.* "Go here. Go there. Now, back here."

Almost before her last word was out, Yiayiá's head shot up, and she made a short, loud raspberry sound and burst out laughing.

"What?" Startled, confused, Kat pointed to the girl on the bag. "Is this Artemis? She's a goddess, right?"

"*Naí,* Artemis is a Greek goddess." Yiayiá shook a flour-covered finger at Kat. "She is hunter, runner. Like you. Is good. Good for you to keep this bag now."

"Okay." Kat patted the *tagári* bag and, even though she didn't get what Yiayiá meant with all the "hunting" talk, gave her a big smile. "Thanks."

"*Efcharistó polý,*" said Yiayiá, then waited.

"*Efcharistó polý,*" parroted Kat.

"*Brávo.*" Yiayiá clapped her hands as if Kat had sung her a song, then picked up four of the small fish and held them out. "This, *marithiá.* I teach you."

Kat hated the thought of the slimy little critters, but Yiayiá's face, bright and inviting, had her putting the *tagári* down and stepping close.

"This way," said Yiayiá, deftly rolling the slim bodies in flour, pinching their tails together, and tossing them onto a wide plate. She held out another four fish. Kat took them between the tips of her fingers and rolled them slowly in the flour, pinching their tails together. When she finished, she held the fish fan out to Yiayiá.

"*Kalá.* Is good," pronounced Yiayiá and, beaming, took the fish.

Kat shrugged and picked up another four fish. "Yeah," she said, surprised that she meant it. "Totally *kalá.*"

Sitting on the swing now, Kat stroked the pattern on the *tagári*, remembering how, later, when Mom saw the bag, she hugged it to her chest and dragged Kat into her and James's bedroom where she hauled a big yellow book of Greek myths out of her suitcase, her face lighting up. The Artemis as Goddess of the Hunt stories were pretty cool, but when Mom started in on the Protector of Virgins stuff? Kat shuddered at the memory, pulling her journal from the bag. There was no way she wanted to listen to Mom—or *anyone* else—talk about virgins.

The front gate squeaked open, and Nikos bounded through, calling at top volume, "Dimitri?"

Behind him came Yeorgia. She shuffled over and perched at the other end of the swing, murmuring, "Good morning."

Before Kat could answer, Theía Tassia breezed through the gate, throwing the two girls a glance as she marched up the patio steps, crowing, "*Brávo!* Yeorgia to speaking English with Katina!" Then she plowed across the patio to where Mom and Yiayiá sat deep in conversation. The minute Tassia plopped down, Yiayiá and Mom stopped talking and gave her twin neon smiles.

Kat twisted to Yeorgia. "Why is Theía Tassia so desperate for you to speak English?"

Yeorgia shot her a quick look. "She want me to learn, eh, for school," she said, as if Kat had asked her why she needed to breathe. "And I am wanting for the future."

"What does *that* mean?"

"*Thélo*—" Yeorgia began, then flashed her shy smile. "*Sygnómi*, Katina—Kat. I want job. For traveling. Like to America."

From the way Yeorgia's eyebrows drew together, Kat could see she struggled to find the right words.

"I know the Wi-Fi here is no good, like for me," said Kat, "but don't you even have a phone? You know, so you could use a translator app?"

Yeorgia laughed and shook her head. "The Wi-Fi is, eh, no good here for us, and my mother . . . she no want this. In Paralia."

"I hear that." Kat sighed and gestured for Yeorgia to continue, saying, "Tell me more about this job you want."

After a moment, Yeorgia swung out her arms, shifting her body side to side, flying.

Kat sat up. *Ooh, charades.* "You want to work for the airlines? Like a—a flight attendant?"

"*Óchi*," said Yeorgia, shaking her head. She put her hands together, holding a steering wheel now, then flew her arms again. "*Pilótos.*"

"Pee—? Oh, you want to be a pilot?"

"*Naí, naí.* This," said Yeorgia, smiling big. "A pilot."

Wow! Kat goggled at Yeorgia, embarrassed at how surprised she was that her quiet little cousin had such a huge dream.

The next moment, with a burst of bickering talk and loud scrapes, James and Nikos came around the side of the house, lugging the half-inflated carcass of the yellow raft. Kat circled her finger next to her head. "Those two are crazy."

"Is true," said Yeorgia, nodding and giggling.

"James is *really* crazy," Kat went on. "He wants to be all Greek now. He told me not to call him James anymore. He's *Dimitri.*"

"Yes," said Yeorgia, "my name, Yeorgia, in English is Georgia."

"Like my name is Katherine."

"*Óchi*, no. Katina is . . . is *like* Katherine." Yeorgia pursed her lips. "But is a short name. Like, Kathy, Katie."

"You mean my name isn't even a whole name?" Kat let a short, sharp breath escape. "Figures I only have half a Greek name."

"*Sygnómi*, Katina, I—"

"No, no. Don't be sorry."

Kat shifted her gaze, shutting out her cousin's sad face. Through the weave of bushes beyond Yeorgia's head, bright spangles of blue sea gleamed. Her next words simply tumbled. "What's the English name for . . . Theofilus?"

"Theofilus? Who is Theofilus?"

"What? Oh, no one." Kat tugged at her braid. "I-I heard the name and wondered if there was an English version."

Yeorgia didn't say anything but then did a fast swivel to Mom, calling out, "Theía Maria?"

Breathless, on fire, Kat watched as in slow motion all three women turned toward the swing. She willed her face to stay blank while Yeorgia sang out, "Theía Maria? Katina"—and then a chirping stream of Greek ending with "Theofilus."

Mom spoke to the others, and they conferred in an even faster crush of language.

"There's really no English name for Theofilus," Mom answered finally. "It means 'friend of God' or 'friend of the Gods.'" She threw Kat a questioning look. "Why do you ask, sweets?"

"No reason. I heard that name, um, maybe at the airport? And you know"—she brushed the end of her braid over her lips—"wondered."

Mom raised her eyebrows before turning back to Yiayiá and Tassia.

Kat slumped against the swing, her body stinging from hearing them say *Theofilus* over and over. Still, *friend of the Gods*. She flipped open her journal, wanting to write the words next to his name.

"Katina?" Yeorgia squeezed Kat's arm, her voice low and hot. "I did something wrong? *Sygnómi*, I—"

"No. No. It's no big deal. Forget it." Kat clapped the journal shut. Better to save her friend of God for when she was alone. "Hey, tell me more about the pilot thing. Do your parents . . ." She trailed off. *What was that weird grunting noise?*

She craned her head. Through the scrub of bushes behind the swing, and beyond the stretch of a narrow strip of empty lot, was the side porch of Kyría Marula's house. There, reclining on a padded bench, was a kid grunting away as he struggled to push up a barbell from his chest. Worse, he wore nothing but what looked like a black bikini bottom and, lying that way, his boy-parts stood out framed for show.

Gah! Was this Marula's grandson? Mom told her he'd dropped by the day before, but Kat had missed him because that was when she'd been in town with Yiayiá. What was his name? Miguel? Manuel?

She turned to ask, but Yeorgia was in hysterics. Kat cracked up hard, too, and soon both girls writhed against the swing seat.

Kat pointed to her own bathing suit bottom. In her jokiest voice, she said the one Greek word she could think of, *oraía*, "beautiful," lifting her arm to make a he-man muscle.

Yeorgia's giggles took on the desperation of near pain. "Manolis is"—she sputtered with laughter—"*Herakles*."

Manolis. Right. Kat doubled over, a hulking, cartoonish Hercules-Manolis filling her head.

"Yeorgia?"

It was Manolis. He had to have heard them because he sat up now, facing Yiayiá's house. He called again, his voice thin and reedy, his head moving side to side, hunting.

One hand over her mouth, Kat grabbed Yeorgia's arm, then both girls ducked down, dissolving into the kind of giggles that hurt from trying to keep them silent.

His voice came again. "Yeorgia?"

Kat peeked over the back of the swing. Too tall and too thin, Manolis now leaned over Marula's railing, searching through the bushes, his smile jack-o'-lantern wide.

She caught his eye and, embarrassing as it was to be busted playing peekaboo, sat up and waved. Manolis squinted at her as though he needed glasses, stretching even farther over the railing. Then his smile dimmed a few watts.

"You?" He jerked back. "*You* are Katina?"

Nice "Hello."

Kat sat up taller. She should probably say "Hi" back, but what was with these gawking Greek men? First that fisherman-guy, and now Manolis? Except Manolis stared at her as if she were not only an alien, but one about to zap him with a ray gun.

For one long, weirdly frozen moment, the two of them blinked at each other, neither moving, then Manolis's face went sleepy and relaxed, his mega smile returning. "Eh . . . hello." He rested his elbows against the railing. "I cannot believe this is you. I—"

"Girls?" Yiayiá poked her head between theirs. "Who you are talking to?"

Before either Kat or Yeorgia could answer, a high-pitched

yelp erupted from across the lot. Tiny, kerchiefed Marula flew at Manolis, buzzing around him like a demented hummingbird, full-on scolding him while attempting to drape a shirt over his bare back. One of his hands clutching at the shirt, Manolis seemed to be trying to talk to her, his other hand pumping up and down in a calm-down motion. Then he pointed toward Yiayiá's house.

Marula broke off mid-scold, her head spinning. When she spotted Yiayiá, she called out, "Sofia!" and her complaining cut razor-sharp across the lot.

Yiayiá answered, her words coming out slow, apologetic.

What was going on here? Kat's gaze swept from Yiayiá to Marula to Yeorgia. And hey, what was with Yeorgia's guilty face?

A moment later, Marula gave Yiayiá a stiff nod and dragged Manolis into the house.

"Well." Kat let out a small laugh. "That was—"

Before she could say another word, Theía Tassia swooped to the swing, hammering questions at Yeorgia. Mom was right on her heels.

"What is all this racket?" Mom turned to Yiayiá. "Mamá?"

Tassia cut in front of Yiayiá, launching a tirade at Mom; the finale, a finger pointed at Kat.

Shaking her head, Yeorgia grabbed her mother's arm. "Óchi, Mamá!"

Whatever Yeorgia said next had the effect of an exploding bomb. Tassia, her face pinched, yanked Yeorgia up from the swing and marched her down the patio stairs and out the gate.

Sheesh! What was the big deal? Sure, they'd been poking a little fun at Manolis, but they hadn't *done* anything. Kat's eyes darted to the weights sitting on Manolis's now-empty bench. Unless he—

Her head jerked up at Mom's hand on her shoulder.

"Kat? What were you and Yeorgia thinking?"

"What? We weren't thinking anything. We were kidding around, you know, getting to know each other like you wanted."

"I'm glad you're getting along, but Tassia's very upset. Marula told Yiayiá you and Yeorgia were spying on Manolis, making *inappropriate* jokes about him."

Inappropriate—what? Heat prickled in Kat's chest. She opened her mouth to defend herself, but Mom talked on. "Yeorgia said she started things, but I can't believe that. She would never be that rude. You have to understand, Greek girls don't—"

"I'm not a Greek girl," Kat said, shrugging Mom's hand away, knowing even as she said the words that they would hit harder than she wanted them to. She worked to lower her voice. "Yeorgia didn't do anything and neither did I."

"I'm not saying you *did* anything, but we are in a place where things—manners—are different and—"

"We weren't doing anything!" Kat's fist hit her thigh with each word. "It's not my problem if nobody here gets that."

"It's not supposed to be a problem." Mom cocked her head, her mouth relaxing to a thin curve. "Look, I'll talk to Tassia. I know she's glad you and Yeorgia are making friends. And you know there's nothing I want more than for you to get along with everyone here. But c'mon, sweets, you're fully old enough to be more thoughtful about how different a lot of the customs can be."

"Maybe you should have thought of that before dragging me here." Kat crossed her arms, trying to keep them and her voice from shaking. "Maybe you should have thought of that before you gave me a half-Greek name and a no-Greek life."

Mouth slightly open, Mom stared at her as though she didn't recognize her anymore. Kat spun away only to catch Yiayiá watching her with a sad, deflated little smile, the kind that made everything a gazillion times worse.

"I'm really starting to get why Dad never wanted to visit this place," Kat said, snatching up the *tagári*. "I'll see you all later."

CHAPTER FIFTEEN

K at dashed over the hot pebbles of the beach and dropped, dripping and breathless, onto her towel. She settled back on her elbows, basking in how the intense heat of the air made her wet skin vibrate with cool. Then she gazed at the sea. A short way out, James and Nikos frolicked on their now-fixed raft, taking turns doing cannonballs off the side. They'd invited her to join them, but . . . Kat picked at the pebbles. Maybe she would in a minute.

Besides, being here on the beach was okay—good even. Tasty as a perfectly ripened peach. She fished into the *tagári* for the peach she'd grabbed at breakfast. Taking a bite, her eyes traveled along the beach and all the way to the town end of the bay. She could just make out the flagpole sticking up beyond the rock jetty. Her head spun in the other direction. Far, far to the edge of this side of the bay, two dusty tan and greenish humps of scrub-covered land rose up, long and round as beached whales. At the top of the farther-out hump stood a tumbled wall of bleached golden stones circling a tall, crumbling arch.

Wow. That temple, or whatever it was, had to have been there for years. Lots of years. It was in ruins now, but there it was.

Kat nibbled at her peach and, even as her teeth ripped into the fruit, letting out a sweet, spicy tang, a silence filled her, as if she'd dropped through a hole in time. Or no—more like that long-ago time was still here, now, with her on this beach. It was just . . . just so *quiet*. Except for a family about a mile away to her right, two guys kicking a soccer ball way, way to her left, and the clone cousins out on the raft, she had the whole beach to herself.

This was what she needed. To think on her own, *be* on her own, without everyone staring at her and clacking away about Greek this and Greek that. Again, she heard Mom going off about "good Greek girls." What was that scene at Yiayiá's even about? One minute she and Yeorgia were sitting on the swing laughing about nothing, and the next, Theía Tassia was freaking out. And what about Mom? What was she trying to prove with this trip anyway? Kat took another bite of peach. Then, to top everything off, Yiayiá hadn't wanted her to go anywhere by herself, and *bang*—now she had to beach-sit the clones.

Kat licked peach juice from her salty lips and squinted toward where the boys floated. Sparkling water rippled against the yellow rubber of the raft, making her think of boats. Of fishing boats. Of what Theofilus might be doing out on his.

She tried to picture his face but could conjure only a blur of tanned skin and dark hair bursting out of the sea.

The sea. Aegean. Blue.

She dragged her wet braid over her shoulder and lay back on her towel, closing her eyes. What made the water that incredible blue? Not the sky. It was pale, almost white. Her fingers itched for her phone and the power to search online. Maybe she'd ask Yeorgia later. That is, if Theía Tassia would let Yeorgia talk to her. She thrust away the image of Theía Tassia's harpy face, and her brain went slippery as the sun made blue and orange and black pulse inside her lids.

A shadow across her face made the colors chill and darken. Her eyes snapped open to the looming silhouette of a boy.

Theofilus!

Sun-dazzled, her heart almost booming through her chest, she sat up fast while a towel fluttered down, overlapping the edge of hers.

"Katina? Hello."

Not Theofilus.

Disappointment was a swift, hot knife. It was Weightlifter-Boy from next door. Manolis.

"I may join you?"

Without waiting for a reply, he tossed down a magazine and a bottle of sunscreen and dropped to her right. "I am Manolis. You met my *yiayiá* before? Marula?"

Kat opened her mouth, but everything about him—his toothy smile, his shiny long-sleeved shirt, his gangly body—crowded her. She couldn't speak.

"I am sad I don't meet you yesterday morning." He hesitated, his smile fading a little as he searched her face. Then, eyes skittering away, he continued, words racing out of his mouth. "But you are not home, and then I have many things to do and . . ."

Mom wasn't kidding. The guy could speak English. Lots of English. Kat waited for him to get to the morning's trouble, but he didn't, instead jumping from one topic to the next like a nervous frog. Now, he was telling her why he was at Marula's.

"I tell my parents I don't want to paint Marula's shutters this summer, but they make me come here to do it. Is very boring this job, and Marula wake me too early. Also, she want the same color like every house here." He made a scoffing sound, holding out his hand to show her a smear of blue paint on the back. "Always this blue. Is very dull."

So, he felt stuck in Paralia, too. Kat wanted to be sympathetic, but the long-suffering tone he used when he talked about Marula and her painting needs put her off. And why did he keep darting glances at her, at her chest to be exact, as though peeking from behind a tree?

Besides, even if she wanted to be sympathetic, she couldn't be: the guy's mouth never stopped moving.

"That's Paralia. Everything here is dull. No internet, no phone, no computers, no movies. Is nothing like America." He shot her a half smile, fully expecting her to nod in agreement.

She couldn't. Everything he said, and was still saying, was what she'd been thinking over the last couple of days, but hearing him say the words out loud as if he could see inside her head made her twisty, uncomfortable.

Even so, she couldn't help studying him as he spoke. Up close his hair was wavy and dark, the type that always looked unwashed, and his face had that thin softness that made him look girlish. Behind his half-unbuttoned shirt, a slice of his chest showed, milky and pale, like a bar of soap with a few scraggly hairs stuck to it. *Yech and blech.* At least he wasn't wearing that black bikini thing.

"In a few weeks. When I'm done here. I go back to Athens and work for my father. He own two jewelry stores. You see this?" All puffed up, Manolis tugged a thick gold chain from behind his shirt collar. "Is very nice, right? I can get any kind of necklace or ring. Better than in America. You tell me what you like and—"

"About this morning." Her voice came out louder than she intended, but him offering her jewelry—on top of talking her ears off—pushed her over an invisible edge. "What was that all about? I mean, what did you say to your grandmother that made her that mad?"

Manolis froze, his fingers tangling in his necklace. "I say, eh, nothing." Carefully, he tucked the chain back under his shirt collar. "Marula? She is very old-fashioned. She tell me I need to be a good host for you. Paralia is very dull, but I show you around. Show you Greece. You like Greece?"

"Sure," Kat managed. *All that yelling was Marula being old-fashioned?*

"Good, that's good. You know"—Manolis leaned closer—"I meet you before. When you visit here long, long time ago. A little girl only. But I am seeing you don't remember me."

Kat bent back, the perfumy smell of too much aftershave settling thick as a cloud around her head.

"You're right. I don't remember you."

"You are different now. Very tall. The first time I see you, I don't remember you." He snickered, eyes flicking over her again. "I think you are a Dutch girl."

Dutch? Tall? Kat frowned. They'd been sitting here only a few minutes. Where was he getting this stuff?

She glanced toward the road, hoping that Mom or Yeorgia or any of the other relatives had decided to come to the beach. *Nope.* She turned to the sea. James and Nikos floated even farther out than before, their heads perched on the puffed side of the raft like tiny lazy turtles sunning themselves on a log.

Were they out too far? She leaned forward, shading her eyes with her hand. Maybe she should yell at them to come in. Yeah, it was time to get back to Yiayiá's.

Pressure on the back of her shoulder startled her.

"You are burning." Manolis pressed her with his finger again. "See?"

Mesmerized, incredulous, she stared at the bony length of

his finger touching her skin, the spot on her shoulder going white, then pink.

"Here." Manolis picked up his sunscreen. "I put some on you."

"No." She scrambled to her knees. "That's okay."

All at once a soccer ball bounced hard off her calf, landing with a *thump* next to Manolis. The air filled with loud yells of "Eh, Manolis" and "*Sygnómi*," followed by laughter and the sharp crush of feet running on pebbles.

The two boys who'd been playing soccer down the beach threw themselves down on Kat's other side. She was surrounded.

Older than Manolis by at least a couple of years, both boys gabbled away in loud, fast Greek, their eyes racing over her. She sat back and drew her knees to her chest, digging her toes into her towel until they chafed against the pebbles beneath.

"Kat?" Manolis's voice practically warbled with excitement. "This Michalis. This Efthimios."

"Hi," she said, pasting on a smile and giving them a stiff little wave.

She didn't like the way they stared at her, as if she were a shiny new sports car.

Oh, lighten up! For a flashing second, her friend Angie whispered into her ear. *Hello? High school guys?*

The one sitting closest—Michalis?—angled his head toward her. "You are American. I love America."

Efthimios leaned over his friend. "We go there two, three weeks? No, eh, months? *Éla, vre* Manolis . . ." He kept talking, gesturing to Kat.

"Efthimios say he and Michalis will go to America in three months," said Manolis, clearly enjoying that the other boys needed him to translate. "They want to know about your life. In America."

"Uh, there's really nothing to know."

Manolis made a comment, and both boys burst out laughing.

"*Éla*, Kat." Efthimios wagged his finger at her. "We know American girls."

Kat gathered her knees closer, frowning at the intimacy of his tone. "W-what?"

"American TV. Hollywood. Social media." He offered her his version of a movie-star smile, then spoke to Michalis.

She turned to Manolis. "What is he talking about?"

Manolis didn't look at her, instead picking at the paint on his hand. "He say American girls are very . . . free."

"Free?" She glanced from Efthimios to Michalis, noticing for the first time how sharp their teeth looked. "Free from what?"

Michalis spoke to Efthimios, and then Manolis joined in, saying something about Marula that made all three of them crack up.

Ha, ha, so funny! Would these guys ever share the joke?

"Kat? Eh, Michalis live near here," said Manolis. "His house is very big, very nice. He want to invite you to come. To see his house."

"You mean now?"

"*Naí, tóra.* Now," said Michalis. He reached across her to grab up the soccer ball, all ready to go.

"I can't. I-I have to babysit." She tried to spot the raft on the stretch of sea beyond Michalis and Efthimios, but sun flashing on the surface blinded her, making her blink and squint. "My brother and my cousin are—"

She jerked back when Michalis leaned across her again to speak to Manolis.

"He say we can come this afternoon," Manolis chirped. "To play cards, maybe."

"No, I can't." Kat faced Manolis, frowning. "Hey, I thought afternoon was the *siesta* time. You know, the big nap?"

"Yes, but he say his parents in Athens today and—"

Michalis interrupted him, and then all three boys talked at once. The word *siesta* came up, and Michalis and Efthimios let out twin dirty laughs, watching her.

What? Fast as flame—*American girls, free, no parents, siesta-nap-sleep*—blazed through her head. Worse, she was the one who'd brought the *siesta*-thing up! She looked at their smug faces, and the hair along her arms shivered as if her skin shrank.

"I have to go," she said, hurrying to her feet, scooping up the *tagári* and her towel.

Manolis looked up at her, his eyes narrow slits. "But we just get here."

"Yeah, I know. It's . . ." Her gaze shot to Efthimios and Michalis, their self-satisfied grins infuriating her. A scene from her FastGrlz book burst into her head. "It's—girl stuff."

"What?"

"Girl problems," she went on, "you know, the old plumbing."

Manolis's eyes went wide as though she'd flicked him on the forehead.

"Tell your *friends*," she said, nudging her chin toward the others. "Well, gotta go."

She strode away, instantly gritting her teeth when the smash of scattering pebbles behind let her know that one, maybe two, of the boys followed. *Perfect.* Now they were calling her name, making idiot hooting noises. She marched faster.

Thankfully, the clamor behind stopped, then retreated. She shuddered, hating how relieved she was. *Jerks!*

Far enough away now, she slowed and, hauling the *tagári* strap over her head, caught sight of the Artemis figure.

"Some Protector of Virgins," she said under her breath.

She shook her head, letting out a small laugh. And had she actually quoted her dumb book? Using her period as a gross-out weapon? The look on Manolis's face gave her a tiny pang, but—*served him right*. He should've stuck up for her, then she wouldn't have had to sit through all that—all that bull *skatá*!

When she reached the road, she whipped around. *God!* She'd forgotten all about James and Nikos. She scanned the sea, the beach. No sign of the boys or the raft.

CHAPTER SIXTEEN

The drive to town took forever. In the front seat, Theíos Nick, Theía Tassia, and Mom sat shoulder to shoulder, the fierceness of their purpose as tangible as if their bodies were nailed together. Kat rode in back, cinched between Yeorgia and Yiayiá. No one said a word except Yiayiá, who kept up a constant flow of chatter to the three in front.

"It will be okay," Yeorgia whispered to Kat. "At the market, there is Wi-Fi. We can call for rescue."

Kat nodded, one finger twisting and untwisting around her braid. She kept seeing James and Nikos in the raft. Right out in front of her. Then the raft vanished, as if a giant sea creature swallowed it whole.

After she'd realized the boys had disappeared, time slowed to a crawl. Years went by while she ran up the hill to Yiayiá's to report the boys missing, and then more years for Mom and Yiayiá to fetch Tassia and Yeorgia and Nick. Trapped by motion and yelling and Greek, there was nothing for Kat to do except follow, and sweat, and follow some more.

Briefly, they'd stopped by the beach, and Kat couldn't help but notice that Manolis and his idiot friends had left.

Then, when Theíos Nick swept the horizon with binoculars, Mom had asked her where she last saw the boys.

Kat pointed toward the twin humps of land and the ruins at the end of the bay, but she hadn't been sure, and her gesture felt like a lie. Probably because she'd already lied. After what had happened on the patio that morning, she couldn't admit that Manolis and his friends had distracted her from watching the boys. Instead, she told Mom she'd fallen asleep.

What did it matter what she'd been doing anyway? James and Nikos were missing and she was at fault. Between Mom's shocked silence and Theía Tassia's high-pitched panic, that was one truth they could all agree on.

At last, Theíos Nick pulled up in front of the market, and with a rush of creaking vinyl and slamming doors, everyone hurried out of the car and into the market. Except Kat. She grabbed Theíos Nick's binoculars and jogged to the jetty.

Quick and stumbling, she made her way along the jagged rocks. When she had a clear view of the bay, she raised the binoculars to her eyes. Pale sky and blue sea filled her vision. James and Nikos had to be out there. Had to be! She twisted one way, then the other, eyes glued to the lenses, the kaleido-scope of images—land, beach, rocks, ruins, water—zipping in and out of sight, dizzying her. But where were they? Where?

In a flash, the jarring smack of a too-close-up object zoomed into view. She adjusted the binoculars, making out a boat, coming closer at a fast clip, and was that—? Yes! A bit of saggy yellow raft poked over the boat's railing.

Kat sprinted for the market, but when she saw Yeorgia com-ing out the door, she yelled to her about the boat and swerved toward the docks.

She leaped down onto the docking and, as the boat chugged in, caught sight of a small dark head. Then there were two heads. Two identical heads.

Everything in her soaring, Kat rushed along, calling out, "James! Nikos! Hey, you guys!"

"Kat? Katina!" Both boys jumped over the boat railing onto the dock.

Half crying, half laughing, she alternately hugged them and smacked at them. "You dumb idiots. Why did you go out that far?"

"We couldn't help it," said James, "we yelled and yelled."

"I didn't hear you, and then you guys were totally gone."

"That's 'cause you were busy with those stupid guys and—"

"I wasn't—"

A crusty half cough made Kat whip around. Stepping off the boat was the man who'd saved the boys.

"Thank you so much," Kat said, launching herself at him. "I mean, *efcharistó. Efcharistó polý!*"

The second she grabbed his hand, Kat knew she'd made a mistake. She let go, fell back.

The fisherman's ancient face, creased and leatherlike, dipped, giving her a quick up and down, making her instantly tug the hem of her suddenly too short T-shirt. It didn't even come close to covering her suddenly too small bikini bottom. *Uh-oh.* She knew that face. It was the face from the morning before. The face that had looked at her with this same expression of disapproval and—the connection fired in her brain a second before another body appeared.

Theofilus.

He stepped onto the dock, his gaze spinning her like a top.

The rest of the family was on them then, talking, scolding, laughing. And meeting the rescuers: Kýrios Zafirakis and his grandson, Theofilus.

"Theofilus?" Mom twisted fast to Kat. "Didn't you ask about a Theofilus?"

"W-what?" Kat choked out a laugh she hoped sounded confused, her eyes darting away only to land on Kýrios Zafirakis's storm-cloud face. Heat flushed through her, but then Yeorgia scurried in front of her and grabbed Nikos's head, saying, "Ach, Mamá! Theía Maria! Po, po, po."

Still talking, Yeorgia pointed to Nikos's eyes, then did the same to James's. Whatever she was saying—the only word Kat understood was kókkino, "red"—sucked the grown-ups' attention, including Mom's, back to the boys.

Kat shuffled back from the commotion and peeked at Theofilus. He tied one of the boat's stern lines to the dock, only a couple of steps away, a couple of steps that yawned as wide as an uncrossable chasm. Had he heard Mom going off about all the name stuff? His eyes hid any answer under his lashes. More than anything, she wanted to talk to him, but then everyone would gawk at her again.

One quick motion and he stood smack in front of her.

"Yassou," he said, holding out his hand.

She put her hand in his, watched their fingers clasp. Whoa.

Her gaze caught his, and like a rogue wave, the reason they were all on the docks hit her again.

"Oh my God!" She couldn't stop shaking his hand. "Thank you so, so much for bringing James and Nikos back."

He smiled big, looking over to the boys, returning to her. "Pos se léne?"

"What?"

He extracted his hand gently from hers, and pointed to himself. "Theofilus," he said, then pointed at her, repeating, "Pos se léne?"

"I'm Kat. Kat Baker," she said, laying her palm on her chest. His smile grew. "Kat? Ti eínai Kat?"

His forehead crinkled as he spoke, and a lock of his hair fell across his cheek. She wanted to reach up and brush it back, actually had to press her hand against her leg to keep her fingers from moving. What was this? She had to get a grip. Control herself. But wait—he was asking her a question.

"What? I—I don't speak Greek."

He watched her mouth as she spoke, shook his head, and said more in Greek. Confusion prickled at her.

"Do you," she said, pointing at him, "speak"—she made her fingers act out words coming from her mouth—"English?"

"English?" Theofilus chuckled. He shook his head, his expression wistful now. "Óchi."

The moment before she heard "Óchi," Kat knew what she already suspected. Theofilus—Theofilus of the deep brown eyes—didn't speak English.

A large, calloused hand went around Theofilus's shoulder. His grandfather. He murmured to Theofilus, patting at his bicep. Kat caught the word American. *Was he talking about her?* Since Theofilus didn't smile anymore, whatever he said wasn't positive. Kýrios Zafirakis directed another probing glance her way and tugged at Theofilus.

Theofilus didn't move, commenting to his grandfather before turning back to her.

"Kat." He held up a finger, asking her to wait.

She kept her eyes on him as he and Kýrios Zafirakis joined Theíos Nick on the boat, hoping whatever they needed to do, they'd be quick. Then she and Theofilus could . . . could what? How could she even talk to him?

Theofilus disappeared into the boat's pilothouse, and Kýrios Zafirakis and Theíos Nick carried the raft over to the dock, Kýrios Zafirakis gesturing broadly, all the while talking to Theíos Nick. Theíos Nick shook his head, said something. Then he pointed to her.

Kat swallowed hard, her insides fuzzing and chilling. They had to be discussing how the boys got lost. More specifically, how she was supposed to be watching them at the time.

Yup. Kýrios Zafirakis threw her a sharp glance, his forehead puckering into a series of disgusted Vs.

Theofilus reappeared, handed what looked like a tool to his grandfather, and moved by, heading her way.

"Theofilus!" The smack of Kýrios Zafirakis's voice was a slamming door.

Horror-movie slow, Kat watched Theofilus turn to his grandfather. She couldn't see either of their faces anymore, but when Theofilus's shoulders slumped, she knew what would happen next.

Theofilus looked over his shoulder, his expression wistful again.

"*Antío,* Kat."

CHAPTER SEVENTEEN

That evening, when the sun was solidly down, Kat hurried to her room. From the moment she and the family had left the docks, it had been as though scalding bubbles boiled and popped in her belly. *What a horrible, stupid day!* The only thing that would make anything better was running—and that's what she was going to do.

After yanking on her running gear, she plopped to the bed to put on her shoes and paused, her fingers trembling as she peered up at the window. It wasn't even dark yet, wouldn't be for a little while, so why was she this worked up? She took a breath. She had plenty of time to go for her run. Plenty of time before full dark.

She took another breath, let it out long and slow. The misery of the day. That's what tore at her. Sure, she actually met Theofilus, but—but *gah!* The way his grandfather looked at her.

Forget about it. Forget about it and this place.

She jammed on her shoes, tying the laces into tight double-knotted bows, and leapt up to do a few quick stretches. When she finished, she swigged from her water bottle, filling her mouth and washing the liquid across her teeth before swallowing. With one last twist of her braid elastic, she stepped out onto the patio.

Mom, James, and Nikos sat together at the big table, heads bent over a book. Yiayiá stood opposite them, the rag she used to wipe the vinyl tablecloth making a slow *swish-swish*. They all glanced at Kat.

"Where are you going?" said Mom.

"For a run," said Kat, reaching her arm over her head for a side stretch.

"*Ti?*" said Yiayiá. She stopped wiping, looking from Mom to Kat.

Mom said a couple of words, and Yiayiá faced Kat, clicking her tongue.

"*Óchi.*"

Hands parked on her hips, Yiayiá kept talking, her meaning clear. Kat couldn't go for a run now.

"I'm only going for an hour," Kat said, rounding on Mom. "Tell her it's okay."

"Mamá . . ."

Kat watched Yiayiá's face as Mom spoke, but Yiayiá's expression was set in stone.

"No," Yiayiá said, this time chopping the hand that held the rag like a judge's gavel. "You go. In the day." She patted Kat's arm as she walked by her to go back into the house.

"It really is too late to go out, sweets," said Mom, "especially alone. Why don't we—"

"When am I supposed to run?" Kat said, her voice revving. "It's too hot during the day. So, when?"

"James," said Mom, looking first at James and then at Nikos. "Why don't you and Nikos go get the cards? There's a deck in the bedroom."

James offered Kat a sympathetic glance before he and Nikos shuffled away from the table.

Mom patted the bench beside her. "Come here."

Kat dropped into one of the chairs instead and faced Mom.

"We are only here for a few weeks," Mom began, her voice low, "and you are a smart girl. I am sure you can figure out how to get exercise during the day. Why don't you try swimming?"

"Because I'm not a swimmer," Kat said, crossing her arms tight. "I'm a runner. Because I want to run on the cross-country team, like I told you. To do that, I have to be able to run. And I can't run in this—this stupid, idiot Greek heat!"

"Calm. Down." Mom took a deep breath. "Look, there is nothing I can do about the heat. But come on. After what happened with the boys today, give me a break here."

"I already apologized for what happened about a thousand times, but it's not my fault no one told me to watch out for rip currents. And, hey, even if there *was* a sign, guess what? I wouldn't have been able to read it. *Jeez!* None of that has anything to do with me needing to go for a run right now anyway."

"I already told you. It's almost dark, and Yiayiá—"

"Do *not* tell me this is something else 'good Greek girls' don't do."

"That's not what I was going to say, but yes, 'Greek girls' don't go wandering around after dark, and whether you like it or not, you are half Greek and we are in Greece. So, regardless of following the customs here, I don't want you to go out alone this late."

"Well, that's kind of too bad," Kat said, pushing away from the table. "This is the only time I can go."

"You're right. That is too bad, and you're not going because—you're grounded."

What? "You—you *cannot* be serious! You cannot ground me for what happened with James and Nikos."

"That's not why you're grounded." Mom shook her head, her expression dull in the shadowy light. "I was going to wait to talk to you about this until after James went to bed, but since you're pushing it . . ."

This. Was not. Happening.

"Yes," Mom nodded, "I can see from your face you know exactly what I'm talking about. Telling me you were *napping* when you were fooling around on the beach with a bunch of strange boys? You know how I feel about lying, Kat."

God, this was impossible. "I-I didn't mean to lie and I was not fooling around with any boys. They came over and they were being jerks and—and I left. Then when I looked for James and Nikos, they were gone."

"Why didn't you say that in the first place?"

"Because I knew you'd freak out."

"*That's* why you decided to lie?" Mom blew out a sharp breath. "This is exactly why you cannot go wandering around by yourself. Especially at night."

Kat gaped at Mom, then dropped her eyes, the events of the day crashing around in her head. "This is *so* unfair."

"Oh, it's more than fair, Katina. You're grounded and that's that."

CHAPTER EIGHTEEN

K at dumped her book on the bed and dropped her still-lit flashlight beside it. She huddled there in the near dark. All was quiet out on the patio. This was not a surprise. Over the past hour, her three housemates had stopped by, a "good night" parade. First James poked in his head, inviting her to help him and Nikos try to patch the raft again the next day. *Ha, ha.* Fat chance Mom and Theía Tassia would let anyone patch that raft ever again.

Then Mom had showed, breezing in to ask if she had any laundry and breezing out with a cool "Sleep well." Finally, Yiayiá made an appearance. When Kat looked up, Yiayiá paddled her arms. "Tomorrow, you swim. Is good." She then pinched Kat's bicep. "*Dynató,*" she said, her voice breathy and impressed, "strong."

Yeah, right. Kat had watched Yiayiá leave and, with a sigh, straightened her legs, staring down at her feet encased in white running socks. Now in the gloom, they glowed as if not attached to her body. Next to one of them, she could barely make out the edge of the *Runner's Journal.* She shoved it with her toe, and it slid to the floor.

Even if she tried to run cross-country in the fall, if she couldn't train, she'd be too far behind; she wouldn't have a chance of making the A-team. For a moment, Mike's face flickered in her mind, disappearing as Theofilus's face flashed bright and clear. She banged her head back against the wall once, then again. *Man! Everything was completely—*

She jerked to her feet, paced to the window and back to the bed. Shoving the flashlight out of the way, she perched on the edge of her mattress. The quiet pressed in, louder than earbuds blasting music.

She eyed the window again. The patio torches had long gone out, and not a speck of sun glow remained in the sky. It was dark, full dark. And late. She pushed the light button on her watch. 10:00 p.m. She held herself motionless. Perfectly motionless. Of its own accord, her gaze cut to the bedside cabinet where the *tagári* sat propped against the shadowed wall. The white wool of Artemis's profile, her bow drawn and ready, gleamed. From a place deep inside Kat, a tiny *click*, almost audible. *Artemis wouldn't sit around moaning about her problems.* Kat let out a shallow breath.

And neither would she.

Fingers shaking, Kat grabbed up her running shoes and slipped them on. *She'd only be gone for thirty minutes.* She stood. *Forty-five, tops.*

She started to go, then reached for the flashlight, flicking it off. The metal weight of it nestled heavy and comforting in her hand. She wouldn't turn it on while she ran, but it would be good to have it in case—*stop!* This was not the time to think of helmet-headed bikers.

She began to ease out through the bamboo curtain, but paused again, swiveling to the window facing the path to the back gate. *Much better.* Skirting the bed, she loosened the screen.

Determined to be quiet, Kat took forever to crunch and stumble across the empty lot between Yiayiá's and Marula's houses and then to climb the chest-high expanse of chain-link fence. By the time she stretched over the scraggly shrubbery growing against the fence and lowered to the road, her breath rasped in and out, a rusty saw. She tiptoed until she was well past Yiayiá's house, then checked her watch. 10:18 p.m. *Okay.* She jogged out to the beach road.

Once she headed down the hill, her breathing came easier. It was definitely darker than on that first early-morning run, but the scorching grip of heat had let go of the day. Kat picked up her pace, glancing up at the pale, silvery moon. It was a bit more than half full and bright enough to light her way. *And look at the sea!* The glitter and wash of moonglow moved over the water like hands waving, urging her on.

A sensation grew inside her, one that made her want to laugh and cry at the same time. She inhaled the night air, thick with the tangy, salty sea smell, and stretched her legs as if she were one of those horses kept in a pen that managed finally to break through the fence, only to take off at a full gallop.

Love the running. Oh, yes. Yes!

In what seemed no time at all, the rock-pile jetty, then the harbor and the town beyond rose up before her. She ran faster, her breath a quick swoop, her legs light and energized. Now she was at the jetty where the rocks loomed like massive, slumbering beasts. Then she was zipping past the harbor, water slapping at the sides of the pitching fishing boats.

She slowed as she approached the buildings. Music pumped from the *tavérna*, nudging her to keep to the dark edge of the road, the shadows. No one could see her, and she wanted to keep it that way.

Through the town she went, moving, always moving. Past the *tavérna*, the market. She glided by the big rock where she'd stopped to stretch that first day. The road changed, began to go up. Up the mountain.

In a blink, whatever the magic spell of breath and muscle that had kept her going evaporated. Kat dragged herself as far up the mountain road as she could, but after only a few minutes, her body screaming, she slowed to a jog, then to a walk, and stopped.

Laboring, gasping, she stuffed the flashlight under her arm and checked her watch. 10:34 p.m. Sixteen minutes and she'd run well over two miles. She lifted her gaze to where she knew the top of the mountain was, then smiled as she walked back the way she'd come. Sixteen awesome minutes, and up until the very end, she'd never run better, stronger, or faster.

CHAPTER NINETEEN

K at backtracked through the town as quickly as her stiffening legs would let her. She wanted to do a few stretches, but standing on the side of a dark road, even in the quiet blue of moonlight, was a lot less welcoming than running on that road.

At the town's center, the tinny beat of *tavérna* music continued to punch the night air, fast and jangly, the Greek lyrics sounding to Kat more like howling than singing.

From her place in the shadows, Kat peered through the loose weave of vines and bushes wrapping around the *tavérna's* latticed patio. The tables near the road were empty, but inside a couple of them were occupied. Mostly by men. Farther in, more men and a few women perched on stools tucked up against a long bamboo bar. Clouds of cigarette smoke blended in with the charcoal tang of lemony grilled fish, and voices—talking, laughing—mixed in and out of the unfamiliar pop music.

Kat's breath came out like a sigh. She'd imagined the *tavérna* as more of a Greek festival, with a bouzouki wailing and circles of people dancing and calling out "*Opa!*"

Laughter burst from the far end of the bar all at once, something about it familiar. *Perfect.* There, slouching on their stools, the boys she'd met on the beach that morning. Efthimios and Michalis.

She shrank away, deeper into the shadows, then froze. A tangle of motorbikes rested in the alleyway next to the *tavérna*. *Did one of them belong to Helmet-Man?*

She took a step, then another toward the alley, her breath hitching loud enough that she pressed her lips together. *Be quiet!* She tiptoed closer. If Helmet-Man's bike was here, would she be able to pick it out? Even now she could hear the motor's whine, buzzing and buzzing, could see the awful, creepy facelessness of his helmet: the shell black and shiny, the reflective visor transforming the rider into a gargantuan, insect-like monster. She shuddered hard, but stepped closer to examine the helmets, her thoughts jumping from Helmet-Jerk to her dive into the sea. To the beach. To Michalis and Efthimios laughing on the beach. Laughing in the *tavérna*. *Wait. What if one of them—*

Loud chatter snapped her attention back to the *tavérna*. Efthimios and Michalis. Now strolling right out the door.

Kat twisted one way, the other, pulse spiking, ready to run but, as though deep sand sucked at her legs, she couldn't move. In the next instant, a voice called.

"Kat? *Yassou.*"

She strode away fast, but not fast enough. Now both of them yammered after her.

"Hello . . . American girl. Kat? *Éla!*"

She ran, instantly hearing the rev of motorbikes kicking to life. *Oh, jeez!* She ran faster, the engines roaring in her ears, coming closer. *The docks!* She swerved hard, leaping onto the decking. Pain knifed into her knees, but she didn't stop, couldn't. She had to hide. She stumbled forward. Pounding feet came after her, and she lunged for the nearest boat, grabbing the railing to launch herself over. A hand grabbed her arm, wrenching her around. The flashlight flew from her fingers as another hand grabbed her other arm.

"Get off me!" She struggled as though they were killing her. "Let go."

"What you doing, pretty girl—"

"*Éla*, Kat—"

"Leave me alone!" She struggled harder, the skin on her bare arms chafing under their grasping hands. They didn't let go, only kept laughing and jabbering, beyond pleased to have caught such a big fish.

Ready to scream her head off, Kat opened her mouth just as a bright beam of light hit her full in the face.

A voice boomed from the dark. "*Ti káneis?*" Then again, quieter now, and familiar. "*Ti káneis?*"

Theofilus.

CHAPTER TWENTY

T he planet stopped spinning, but Kat didn't. She spun with how none of this could be real: she'd tumbled into a fantasy and it starred Dream Theofilus, ultimate rescue-god-of-life.

Both Michalis and Efthimios mumbled curses when Theofilus stepped from his boat to the dock, his flashlight blazing and his tone scolding, bursting the moment. The boys dropped their hands from her, and Kat hurried to Theofilus's side.

The three boys continued to talk, like they were bargaining, Michalis's and Efthimios's voices jokey, reasonable and laced with a healthy dose of *Hey, we have no idea why she was freaking out.*

Kat couldn't stop shivering. She hugged her sore arms around herself, wishing she could slip through the dock's wooden planks, never to be seen again.

Michalis turned to her, his expression innocent. "*Éla*, Kat. Eh, you want ride?"

He was offering her a ride home? As if *that's* all they'd wanted with her?

She shook her head.

Theofilus spoke again and put his hand on her shoulder, his fingers resting light, feathery.

"Aaah," said Michalis, drawing the syllable out long with

discovery. He murmured to Efthimios, and they both snickered, glancing from her to Theofilus.

"*Antío*, Kat. You have good time," they said, and their tone—unmistakable—made her wince.

Yep, they knew all about those "free" American girls. All about them.

CHAPTER TWENTY-ONE

fter Michalis and Efthimios left, Theofilus's hand slid from her shoulder.

"Kat?" He whispered her name, as if waking from a dream only to discover her there.

A motorbike engine revved, quickly followed by another. Together she and Theofilus watched Michalis and Efthimios race by, neither, Kat noted, wearing a helmet.

The engine din faded, and Kat blew out a deep, relieved breath. When she turned, she found Theofilus studying her.

"*Ti?*" He paused, sweeping an arm up and around as though gathering the night. "*Yiatí?*"

Why was she out in the night? Like he'd said them, the words bloomed in her head.

"I . . ." She plucked at her running tank, pointed to her shoes, then pumped her arms and legs, running in place. Theofilus watched, his forehead wrinkling.

"Ah," he said at last, then more in rapid Greek.

Kat followed every word, trying to catch anything familiar. When he said *marathónas*, she put out her hand.

"*Naí,*" she said, nodding fast, "that."

He made an amused sound and pointed up to the moon. "*Yiatí tóra?*"

"You mean, why now?" Kat twisted the tail of her braid around her fingers. "Well, I-I have to run now, *tóra*."

Words, or rather the lack of them, made Kat's throat close up, because Theofilus's face had gone still and unsmiling. An image of Kýrios Zafirakis flashed into her head. *No, no, no.* She had to make Theofilus understand, because even if she never saw him again, she couldn't bear him thinking of her the way his grandfather, Michalis, Efthimios, or any other confused Greek man did.

She started again. "The day, the *iméra*, is too hot." She wiped her forehead and lolled her tongue as if she was a desert traveler, then pointed to the moon.

"*Tóra* is good for running. But Mom and Yiayiá, they don't want me out, *éxo*." She put her finger to her lips, pretending to tiptoe run. "So, I have to sneak out *tóra*." She waved her hand to the night as he had. *Man, this was so lame.* "There's no other way and I—I have to run."

Their gaze locked for a long moment before his eyes shifted to where her clasped hands now pressed over her heart. He nodded as if he understood her perfectly.

Kat blew out an exhausted breath. "Great," she said. Her eyes cut to the road. "I should go. Hey, *efcharistó* again for saving me from those guys. I guess they were being jerks. Jeez, shut up, Kat. He doesn't understand a word you're saying." Freshly disgusted with herself, she backed away. "All right, then. *Antío*."

Before she could take another step, Theofilus put his hand on her arm. "*Óchi*," he said, and then gestured as if sipping from a cup.

He was . . . offering her a drink?

"Wow. That's really nice, but I-I don't know." She glanced back at the road. She didn't hear the motorbikes anymore, but maybe she *should* wait a few more minutes to make sure they were gone.

Theofilus tugged her arm, motioning toward his boat.

"Okay, *naí*," she said, "but only for a little while—*lígo*." She tapped her watch, and pinched her thumb and forefinger together. "Got it?"

He grinned and his warm hand slid to hold hers, making her skin want to fly off her bones.

On his boat, they threaded through the darkened shapes of overturned coolers and draped nets. Kat's nose wrinkled, expecting to be overwhelmed with an oily, musky smell, like standing next to the fish counter at the supermarket. The odor was there, but faded. Mostly, she smelled lemons and pine, and a scent she didn't recognize—sweet and herby.

Theofilus opened the door to the cabin and led her down the stairs.

This wasn't real, wasn't real, wasn't real. The words fuzzed in her brain as she took in the tumbled gloss of hair curling around his head and down over his neck, the smooth curve of his shoulder poking from his ancient and torn sleeveless T-shirt. Her eyes ran down his arm to his hand. To her hand held there. It was a dream.

When they stepped into the cabin, Theofilus turned, spoke, then smiled like he, too, had to keep remembering that she didn't understand him. He let go of her hand, placing his flashlight on the counter, and clicked on a battery-powered lantern. Then he crouched to open a large red-and-white cooler, and the *chunk* of glass bottles rubbing against ice filled the tiny space.

Kat hugged herself, shivering slightly. The boat's cabin was like the inside of a small wooden box, each element arranged to make everything fit.

Theofilus held out two bottles, one brown with white lettering, the other yellow with lemon slices, a twin of the one she'd pulled out of the market's cooler the day before.

She pointed to the familiar yellow bottle.

He smiled right into her eyes, and for a moment she was comfortable and at home, as though she'd been in this tiny boat cabin with him a thousand times. She took the bottle, and when his fingers brushed hers, she had to drop her eyes and stand motionless, the roller coaster in her belly rushing and plunging.

She began twisting the top off her drink and went cold, staring at her hands. *Wait—where was her flashlight?* Her head swiveled to the cabin stairs.

"*Ti káneis?*" said Theofilus.

"What?" She turned his way. "I forgot. I dropped my flash–light."

His blank look had her pointing to his flashlight on the counter. "I dropped mine. There," she said, gesturing up toward the dock. She moved toward the stairs, but Theofilus grabbed her arm, shaking his head. He snatched his flashlight and ran up the stairs.

Alone, she opened her soda, took a long fizzy swig, and gazed around.

There wasn't much to the cabin. A small kitchen held a couple of wall cupboards and a counter standing like an island. Next to the counter, seeming to grow from the caramel-colored wooden walls and floor, a deep red, padded bench wrapped first to a small table piled high with papers and stuff and then to the stern. There, a set of short shutter-like doors—maybe leading to the engine? The bench picked up again on the opposite wall. On that side, a thin blue sleeping bag and a squishy-looking pillow made up a rough bed. Nearby, a worn duffel bag lay unzipped on the floor.

Did Theofilus live here? That had to be what Thula meant when she said he "stay on the boat all the time." Did that mean—Kat's pulse jumped—no, it was too small for Kýrios Zafirakis to live here, too. Besides, Theofilus wouldn't have invited her on the boat if his grandfather was going to show up.

Kat wandered to the table. Jumbled next to the papers were boxes of pens and other art supplies. In the middle sat a large pad, open to a penciled drawing. She dragged the pad closer.

Wow! Double wow! Detailed as a photograph, a pencil sketch of Kýrios Zafirakis stared up from the page. She could barely believe anyone could draw such an exact and amazing picture, but at the same time, she knew Theofilus had.

She studied the lines, both bold and gentle, weaving together to make his grandfather. It was a close-up profile of the older man's head and chest. He was on the boat. Steering the boat. Yes, barely visible at the bottom of the page were his hands holding the knobs on the boat's wheel.

A presence, warm as breath on her neck, made Kat turn. Theofilus stood behind her, his gaze concentrated on the picture. She hadn't heard him return.

"Yours?" said Kat, gesturing from the pad to Theofilus.

"*Naí.*" He held out her flashlight.

"Thanks." She took it and turned back to his picture. "This is . . . it's . . . *oraía.*" *Beautiful.*

"*Oraía?*" Theofilus chuckled, shook his head.

He moved to the side of the table, picking up a pencil.

"*Aftó,* eh, this." He tapped at the picture, then wiggled the pencil as if drawing more.

Kat nodded. The picture wasn't finished.

She put her hand on the edge of the pad and glanced at Theofilus, making like she would turn to another page.

Not amused now, he gave the ghost of a nod.

Skin prickling, she turned the page. Pencil, ink, watercolor. Incredible and intricate scenes and images crammed page after page: the boat, the town, the beach; fishermen on the docks, people buying fish, baskets of fruit in front of the market.

Occasionally she looked up, caught his eye, and they smiled at each other.

Then she came to an image that made everything in her—heart, breath, blood—stop.

A watercolor of a girl standing high on the beach, with Paralia town and the road behind her. She wore running clothes, her hair in a braid. Kat breathed in, a sweet ache blooming in her chest. "This is me."

Her finger reached out, brushing watercolor Kat's face, and Theofilus's finger found hers, the tip whisper-touching the tip of hers. She raised her eyes to his—his dark, velvet eyes—and something in her, warm and luscious, unfurled.

CHAPTER TWENTY-TWO

The smell of baking bread woke Kat the next morning. She breathed deep, opened her eyes, and *whoosh*, like a train racing through a station, everything about the night before, about Theofilus, rushed through her. She had to pull her pillow over her head to muffle the happy noises bursting out.

Last night had been the most incredible night of her life.

The way she'd run—*ha ha*—into Theofilus, totally unexpectedly, totally beyond a dream. Of course, that first bit with Michalis and Efthimios was a nightmare. But then the time on the boat zipped by in about a second.

Kat smiled thinking how she'd pointed to her watch, then to the stairs, trying to tell Theofilus she had to leave. He dropped right down on the bench and put on his shoes. She needed no words to know he would walk her home.

When way too soon they reached the end of Yiayiá's lane, she stopped and he did as well, both understanding at the same exact moment that getting caught would stink.

"Good night," she said, her voice barely a whisper.

"Good night," he parroted back, making her smile.

In the dusky glow of moonlight, he hesitated. She held her breath, but he only grinned at her before backing down the lane, melting into the dark.

Pressing her face into her pillow now, Kat replayed the goodbye moment over and over. She'd been sure he would kiss her. She'd wanted him to. Wanted him to now.

Did he want to? And was there any way he wanted to see her again as much as she wanted to see him?

She checked her watch. *Wow.* Late. He had to be out fishing, but maybe they could see each other later. Or on his day off.

Her technology-free status sinking in, Kat leaned back, her head knocking against the wall.

With no phone or computer—not to mention that pesky little problem of not speaking the same language—how could she get in touch with him?

She saw herself pinning a note to where his fishing boat docked and, immediately, an image of Kýrios Zafirakis finding that note jammed into her head. The way he'd watched her on the docks after the James and Nikos raft rescue. He'd been in some hurry to get Theofilus away from her. Nasty, irresponsible girl that she was.

Kat sank lower on the bed. He simply didn't know her. As soon as he did, he—*that was it!*

She swung her legs over the edge of the mattress and jumped up, promptly tripping over the pile of running clothes she'd left on the floor. She scooped up the bundle, sniffed at it, and wrinkled her nose. *Yuck!* She pulled her sleep shirt up to her nose next. Going to bed runner-sweaty was about the grossest thing she'd ever done. She needed a shower, and everything had to go into the wash. She dumped her running clothes on her sweaty sheets, changed out of her sleep shirt, and then gathered up the whole pile of laundry.

No one was out on the patio, but from deep in the main part of the house came a low voice singing in Greek, then the hollow clatter of china. Yiayiá, probably up for hours already, in the kitchen cooking breakfast. Kat walked around the side of the house and past the outdoor oven. Here, the aroma of baking bread was strong enough to make her stomach growl.

Around another corner and behind the shower she found the laundry tub. Nearby sat the large wicker basket where Mom had told her and James to dump their dirty clothes.

Kat threw her pile into the basket, then paused. Any chance Mom or Yiayiá would notice how sweaty the running stuff was? She stared down at the stinky running gear. *Nah.* Even so, she mixed those things in with the other laundry.

"You're awake."

The words, coming as if out of nowhere, made Kat jerk up. Mom's heavy-lidded, freshly woken eyes regarded her.

"Yeah," said Kat, her gaze darting to the laundry basket, then back to Mom. "I was totally pitted out. And my sheets were all sweaty."

"Come on, Kat. The heat's not that bad at night."

"No, no. You're right. Night's not bad at all. I-I think this T-shirt's too heavy." Kat fingered the material covering her chest. "Or I got tangled up in my sheet, or . . ."

Mom was giving her that screwed-up question-mark face.

Kat took a slow breath and offered up a gigantic smile. "Can I take a shower?"

Mom raised the steaming mug she held to her mouth and blew on it, her gaze falling to the now overflowing laundry basket. She didn't take a sip, pursing her lips instead.

"You can take a shower, but we can't wash sheets every day. That's way too much work."

"I could help. With the laundry. Yiayiá could show me how. After my shower."

Mom sipped from her mug, eyeing Kat over the rim, her thoughts as plain as though an LED display ran across her forehead. *What's going on?* those thoughts read. *How is it possible for my daughter to go from the death funk of last night to the gibbering, helpful bunny-girl of this morning?*

"That would be fine," Mom murmured. "Go ahead. Take your shower, but—"

"Keep it short," Kat finished.

Almost smiling, Mom shot Kat another searching look before turning away.

Kat had to bite her tongue to keep from calling Mom back. *No.* She needed to find the perfect moment to put her get-Kýrios-to-like-me plan into motion. No way was she pushing whatever luck had not only protected her from getting caught with her smelly running clothes, but had also given her a foolproof way to cover her tracks.

Helping Yiayiá with the laundry—*perfect.*

Her hair still wet from the shower, Kat joined James, Mom, and Yiayiá at the patio table for breakfast. Hungry and thirsty, Kat gulped down her juice and then helped herself to a piece of Yiayiá's freshly baked bread. She dipped her knife into the pot of butter, slathered a creamy blob onto the steaming slice, and bit in. Soft bread, hard crust, and dripping, salty sweetness. *Yum!*

"*Éla*, Katina," said Yiayiá, holding out a jar of a dark orange, jammy substance. "*Marmeláda.* You try."

Kat took the jar and raised it to her nose. She didn't recognize the deep syrupy tang.

"What is it?" she asked, looking from Yiayiá to Mom.

Mom took the jar, held it to her own nose. "It's apricot," she said, turning to smile at Yiayiá before handing the jar back to Kat. "I always loved this."

The sight of Mom and Yiayiá smiling at each other, completely at ease, gave Kat a tickle of pleasure. Considering how hard Mom had pushed the Paralia trip, she'd been mostly plastic-stiff with Yiayiá. And it wasn't only over the Marula incident or the raft thing. *No.* Kat picked up her knife. Mom had been that way pretty much since they'd arrived. Except now, well, now it was as if she was one of those mini-sponge toys that when dunked in warm water softened and expanded. *Hmm.* With an inward shrug, Kat spread a little of the *marmeláda* on her bread, took a bite. A burst of tart sweetness mixing with the salty cream of the butter exploded on her tongue.

"Wow. This is awesome."

Yiayiá laughed her little-girl laugh and made a comment that had Mom laughing, too.

"Hey," said James. "Let me try some."

Kat took another knife full of *marmeláda* before passing the jar to James. He stuck in his knife and scooped up almost half the contents.

"Jeez, James, I mean, *Dimitri*, leave a little . . ." Kat almost dropped her knife. *Wait. This was perfect.* Slowly, she placed her knife onto the side of her plate. "Hey, you must be *starved* after everything with the raft yesterday."

"Yuh-huh," said James, his eyes narrowing as he concentrated on covering every inch of his bread with *marmeláda*. "I could eat about ten of these."

"I bet." Kat stole a look at Mom and Yiayiá and spoke louder. "How are you feeling after that raft thing, anyway?"

"Fine."

"That was pretty crazy." She tried to make her voice bland, but the words came out breathless and a little shrill. "And how the—the Zafirakises saved you guys? Wow!"

James's face scrunched, his expression saying, *Why are you yelling at me?*

Kat ignored him. "Totally amazing. Don't you think?" She turned to Mom, widening her eyes and shaking her head, newly astounded.

"It sure was," said Mom. "We owe them a lot."

"That is so true." It wasn't hard for Kat to draw the words out, make them smooth as the thick coating of *marmeláda* on James's bread. "You know, we really do owe them a lot. Shouldn't we do something for them? Like, I don't know, invite them over?" She looked from Mom to Yiayiá and took a deep breath. "Hey, I've got a great idea. Let's invite them over for a big 'thank you' feast."

"Why, Kat." Mom's smile rose like the sun. "That is such a nice thought, I—"

"Maria?" said Yiayiá, interrupting.

Kat watched Mom and Yiayiá exchange a few words, then Mom tipped her head back and hooted.

"What?" said Kat, about to explode. "Why are you laughing?"

"Well. It seems that Yiayiá beat us to the punch."

Kat looked from Mom to Yiayiá, lingering on Yiayiá's more-elf-mischievous-than-usual smile. "What do you mean?"

"Yiayiá's already planned a big 'thank you' feast," Mom said, toasting her coffee mug at Kat. "The Zafirakises are coming over for dinner tonight."

CHAPTER TWENTY-THREE

onight. She would see him tonight. Wrapped in her own private golden bubble, Kat spent the morning singing that word in her head. *Tonight,* as she helped Yiayiá water her geraniums. *Tonight,* as she swung laundry up onto the clothesline and later collected it in a basket. *Tonight,* as she marveled again and again that in a few short hours Theofilus would be walking through Yiayiá's gate.

How was it possible? Even now, tucked into the tiny kitchen cooking for the feast, Kat could barely believe that Yiayiá had actually invited the Zafirakises over. But she had—right there on the docks during all the confusion of getting James and Nikos back.

"Katina? *Éla.*" Yiayiá raised a palm full of chopped garlic. "*Skórdo.*"

Kat stopped rolling the fish—*no, the marithiá*—in flour, and dutifully took a whiff.

"*Skórdo,*" she repeated, wrinkling her nose against the pungent burn.

"*Brávo,*" said Yiayiá, dumping the garlic into a pan.

"She's determined to teach you Greek *and* how to cook," said Mom.

"Yeah. You know, I like us, in here, cooking together." Kat

blushed at how Mom beamed at her. "And I-I want to learn Greek." *How about really, really want.* "So far I've got, *lemóni* for lemon, *ntomáta* for tomato, and, oh yeah, *kremmýdi* for onion."

"That's great," said Mom, "you'll be fluent before you know it. Here." She swept the herbs she'd been chopping into a small bowl and followed Yiayiá's example, holding it up to Kat. "*Thymarí*, thyme."

Sweet, minty-grassy. *Mmm.* And strangely familiar. Where had Kat smelled fresh thyme recently?

Last night. She smiled, reaching for another fish. On Theofilus's boat, when he—her lips went numb. Wait. Theofilus hadn't said a *word* about the dinner tonight.

Yiayiá's burst of laughter made Kat look up. Seconds before, Yiayiá had been layering crispy-fried eggplant slices into a casserole dish fast as a Vegas card dealer; now she had one hand on her hip and the other punctuating an animated stream of Greek with a steady *chop-chop.* An instant later, she picked up the casserole dish, blew out a jaunty raspberry, and strode out the back door toward the outdoor oven.

Whoa. Kat turned to Mom. "What was that all about?"

"It's . . ." Amused, Mom shook her head, and sliced into a tomato. "She said she hopes we're all very hungry because she thinks there's a good chance Kýrios Zafirakis will cancel."

The tiny fish Kat held slipped through her fingers.

"It's under the table, sweets."

"W-what?"

"The fish you just dropped." Mom leaned closer, her forehead creasing. "I think you've been in this hot kitchen too long. Your face is flushed."

"No, I-I'm fine." Quickly Kat crouched, more to hide her burning face than to hunt for the fish. "Mom?" she said from under the table. "Why does Yiayiá think Kýrios Zafirakis will cancel?"

"Yiayiá said she had to practically twist his arm to get him to accept her invitation in the first place. That's why she was laughing. She thinks they aren't coming."

Kat froze. Was that why Theofilus hadn't said anything? Because Kýrios Zafirakis didn't bother telling him about a dinner they weren't going to eat?

"He would've let us know by now," Kat said as she stood, the fish clutched in her hand, "if they weren't coming. Because . . . because that would be rude. Totally un-Greek rude to—to just not show up. Right?"

"That's what I told Yiayiá."

"So, *you* think they're coming?"

Mom paused, eyeing her more closely. "You seem awfully interested."

"No. Not really. I mean, we *are* doing a ton to get ready for them. It would stink if they blew us off."

"True," said Mom. "And I do think they'll come no matter how grumpy Kýrios Zafirakis was about it."

"What did he actually say?"

"Oh, something about how he and his grandson are very busy and already lost a day of fishing with the rescue. That they eat most of their meals on the boat while they fish. That they don't have time to entertain tourists. You know, that type of thing."

"How did Yiayiá convince him?"

"She told him that we are not tourists and that we came all the way from America, and used all our money to spend the summer with our Greek family. And," Mom chuckled, "that it would dishonor us if we couldn't thank them with a home-cooked meal."

Kat swallowed, almost choking on a blob of fresh doubt. "I guess he couldn't argue with that."

"He sure couldn't."

Later, Kat headed to the patio swing. All day she'd stashed the memory of how coldly Kýrios Zafirakis had treated her on the docks, but now she couldn't stop thinking about him.

What she wanted was for him to like her—and he *should* like her. Man, she couldn't get more normal. She wasn't pierced or dyed or tattooed. She didn't use bad language. At least none *he* would've heard. The screwup with James and Nikos aside, she was a regular girl, *right?* As regular and parent-pleaser-ish as anybody's grandfather could want.

Kat stretched out on the swing and closed her eyes.

Except maybe stuff that appealed to American grandparent types wasn't the same as what would work with a Greek. Look at how everything had gotten messed up the day before. She squeezed her lids shut tighter. Crap, this was confusing!

The creaking of the gate snapped Kat's eyes open: Yeorgia inched her way through, balancing a large plate in each hand.

"Hi!" Kat hauled herself off the swing and hurried over. "Here, let me help."

Kat took one of the plates and was about to ask Yeorgia where she'd been all day, but Yeorgia hustled by. Frowning slightly, Kat followed her up the steps to the big table.

After they put down the plates, Yeorgia gave Kat a polite, little-old-lady smile and said, "Thank you." The words had barely left her mouth before she raced back down the steps.

What? "Hey, Yeorgia! Wait a sec."

Yeorgia didn't stop until Kat's hand was on her shoulder.

"What's the big rush?"

"I have work." Yeorgia made a half-hearted effort to shrug her shoulder free. "And my mother, she is waiting."

Kat exhaled a long, frustrated stream. "I guess Theía Tassia's still pretty mad at me," she said, wrapping her arm around Yeorgia's shoulder. "I'm super sorry about that, but I really need to talk to you."

She tugged at Yeorgia until they sat on the swing.

"I never got a chance to thank you for sticking up for me with Theía Tassia, you know, about the Manolis thing yesterday. So, *efcharistó.*"

Yeorgia gave her a stiff nod but kept her eyes to herself.

"Okay." Kat fiddled with the end of her braid, staring at Yeorgia's unhappy profile. "Yeorgia? Are you mad at me, too?"

"*Óchi.* Mamá say, 'No talk to Katina. Katina *eínai kakó korítsi.*'"

"Got it. I'm the bad girl. Because of what happened with James and Nikos, right? Man, them getting lost? That really stunk."

"*Naí.* Stunk."

Kat shot Yeorgia a small smile, but Yeorgia still wouldn't look at her.

"Yeorgia. Talk to me."

"James and Nikos . . ." Yeorgia's voice was so quiet that Kat had to slide closer to hear her. "You are not, eh, you have no care to watch them. This scare me very much."

Kat swallowed, her heart shivering as if a window in her chest cracked open, letting in a cold blast.

"I was scared, too." Her shoulders shuddered at the thought of the boys way out on that sinking raft. "And I hope you can understand me, because I know I made a big mistake, and if I could change what happened, I would." She put her hand on top of Yeorgia's. "Can't we be super glad the Zafirakises saved them and—and keep being friends?"

Yeorgia looked at Kat's hand on hers. "*Naí*," she murmured finally, turning her hand palm up to clasp Kat's. "We are friends."

"That's a relief," said Kat, wiping pretend sweat from her forehead.

Yeorgia laughed, then nudged Kat's shoulder. "You like this Theofilus?"

"W-what?"

"You ask about 'Theofilus,' this name. Friend of the gods? And then he is there. This is—"

"Crazy," said Kat, now the one keeping her eyes to herself.

"No crazy. Is *tycherós*. Lucky. But also, I see you like him."

Kat didn't dare look up. Part of her wanted to tell Yeorgia everything about Theofilus, but most of her—not so much.

"*Éla.*" Yeorgia wagged a finger at Kat. "At the dock? When Theía Maria ask you about Theofilus? Your face is very red."

Touching her traitorous cheek, Kat darted a look at Yeorgia. It wasn't like she had to tell her *everything*. "Okay! Okay! Yes. I like him, but fat lot of good that does me. His grandfather hates me."

"What?"

"Kýrios Zafirakis. He thinks I'm a sleazy, lame American girl, a *kakó korítsi* and—man, this is screwed up." Kat shoved at the patio floor with her foot, making the swing jerk. "I want Kýrios Zafirakis to like me. But I don't know how to make that happen."

"You-you want a good impression," said Yeorgia, "for tonight, yes?"

"Yes."

"For guests, I must wear a dress. Look nice. Be nice." Yeorgia shrugged. "This is all."

"That's exactly what I—"

The gate flew open and Theía Tassia came barging through with a huge metal platter.

Yeorgia jumped to her feet, but Kat was quicker.

"Theía Tassia," said Kat, racing down the steps, hands out to take the platter.

Tassia gave Kat a brief nod but marched by without giving up the platter, calling, "Yeorgia!" over her shoulder.

Gulp! Even though Mom said she'd talked to Tassia, Yeorgia's report was the reality. The woman was totally Kat-unhappy.

Kat hurried after her. "Theía Tassia?"

Tassia turned as she put the platter on the table, and Kat had a momentary flash of what a dragon about to spew fire must look like.

"I'm sorry." Kat spun to Yeorgia. "Help me explain this to your mom, okay? Tell her . . ."

What could she say? She didn't want to suck up to Tassia by taking all the blame for the Marula/Manolis incident. And no way was she bringing up what was happening with Manolis and his idiot friends on the beach when James and Nikos disappeared.

"Tell her I feel bad about yesterday—with the whole Manolis/Marula thing. And about James and Nikos. It was all a mistake and-and I apologize for the trouble."

As Yeorgia spoke, Kat watched Tassia's face. Little by little her fierce scowl gentled to a firm non-smile. When Yeorgia finished, Tassia nodded at Kat, and said, "*Entáxei.*" Then she gave Yeorgia what sounded like a couple of orders, pointed at both girls, and strode toward the kitchen.

Kat nudged Yeorgia. "Is everything okay, now?"

"*Naí*," said Yeorgia, her face light and smiling. "Everything good. You come. Mamá want help."

Kat followed Yeorgia, more than ready to do Tassia's bidding.

One dragon down; one to go.

CHAPTER TWENTY-FOUR

K at lay on her bed, staring at her watch. 8:17 p.m. In thirteen minutes—*tick, tick,* now twelve minutes and fifty-eight seconds—Theofilus and his grandfather were supposed to arrive. She scowled at her bare thighs, instantly tugging the hem of her jean skirt lower. Then she smoothed the new Greek top Yiayiá had surprised her with, straightening the puff of sleeve around one wrist, admiring how the Aegean-blue gauze made her skin appear shadowy.

Now it was 8:19 p.m.

She tickled her lips with the tail end of her braid. Maybe she should dress up more, wear her hair down. Or cave and slap on a little of Mom's makeup. Maybe both?

No. She'd fry with her hair spread over her shoulders, and she hated makeup: the gluey smell, the gunky feel, the rubbery taste. Besides, the way Kýrios Zafirakis had glared at first her running gear, then her bathing suit—*Man!* Did she honestly want to find out his opinion of girls in makeup?

Lifting her wrist, she breathed in the one thing of Mom's she had tried: a spritz of orangey, cinnamony cologne. Weirdly enough, even as the smell of dressed-up Mom was familiar and comforting, it made Kat lonely as well. She got quivery, seeing herself small again and back in the old house, hugging Mom before both of her parents stepped out the front door into the dark, off for a big night on the town.

A burst of chatter in the yard made Kat jump to her feet, then her insides fell. Kyría Marula and Manolis. Of course. She should've known they'd be invited.

"*Ach*," said Yiayiá, clapping her hands as Kat appeared. "*Oraía korítsi*."

Beautiful girl? Yeah, right. Kat pasted on a smile and forced herself to walk toward the group. She had to work hard to ignore how Manolis looked her up and down, his too-wide grin telling her he thought she'd dressed up for him.

Then there was Marula. Between thinking of Tassia and Kýrios Zafirakis, she'd forgotten she had to face *this* dragon, too.

"Kyría Marula? Hi. I wanted to apologize—" Kat twisted to Mom. "Will you please tell Kyría Marula how bad I feel about the misunderstanding yesterday?"

Mom blinked at her, her mouth opening in a slight smile. "Why, yes. Of course."

While Mom spoke, Kat focused on Marula, as if she herself was the one making the apology, but she couldn't help stealing a glance at Manolis. Had he figured out that he and his "pals" were the reason she forgot about James and Nikos at the beach? Didn't look like it. Manolis never even looked at James, instead gazing at her as if they shared a secret.

A moment later, Marula, a smile crinkling her whole face, said, "*Éla*, Katina. *Brávo*."

She rattled on and took Kat's hand, held it up, clearly admiring Kat in her Greek shirt. Then she tugged her toward Manolis.

Manolis's stare made Kat want to slink back to her room.

"Marula?" Yiayiá spoke now. "Katina . . ." Yiayiá said a few words that sounded like a request for help, put her arm around Kat, and led her back toward the house.

Kat leaned into the solid warmth of Yiayiá and let out a ragged breath.

"Is okay." Yiayiá gave her a tight squeeze, whispering, "Manolis? No for you. Come. You help me."

Yiayiá left her at the table where a pile of silverware and linen waited.

Yeorgia's family arrived next. They stood in the yard chatting with Mom, Kyría Marula, and Manolis. Except Nikos. He and James ducked around the front of the house, their heads together in their tight world of two.

The gate creaked again, and there was the final dragon—Kýrios Zafirakis. Behind him, Theofilus.

CHAPTER TWENTY-FIVE

Theofilus. The sight of him cut into Kat, hot and sweet. She wanted to rush over, but a flood of too-excited panic held her back. She continued to place napkin, fork, knife, napkin, fork, knife, making sure to fold each napkin in a creased triangle, to align each fork and knife in a perfect pair. As she moved around the table, she spied on the group. Theofilus hadn't seen her yet, he—she bumbled a fork, nearly dropping it. She clutched at the utensil, the metal biting into her palm. *Get. A. Grip!*

When the last knife was in place, there was no choice. She had to say hello. Making her way toward the group, she smoothed her skirt. God, her hands were shaking.

"*Yassou,*" she began. Simultaneously Mom reached for her arm and Theofilus and everyone else turned. Kat dropped her eyes, all the too-close attention overwhelming her.

"*Yassou,*" said Theofilus, his voice breathless. Their gazes met, blazed bright, then skittered away.

"*Sygnómi.*" He talked to Mom now, apologizing while raking freshly showered hair off his forehead and straightening the front of his slightly wrinkled white shirt.

Mom let out a bewildered little laugh, answering him with a "don't worry about it" tone, before whispering to Kat. "He's apologizing for keeping us waiting, except he had *no idea they were coming over.*"

Theofilus cast a fierce, questioning look at Kat. *Jeez!* Here she'd been wondering why he hadn't mentioned the dinner last night, and *he'd been wondering the same thing about her.* She widened her eyes, shrugging the tiniest bit, and when he grinned, she did, too.

Kýrios Zafirakis put an arm around his shoulder, and Theofilus's expression shuttered.

Kat's smile slipped. What was going on between Theofilus and his grandfather?

The elder Zafirakis spoke now. She focused on his mouth, as if watching the words form would help her understand him. Not working. Maybe she should say *efcharistó* about the rescue again, or—a picture flashed into her head, of her offering him a cool drink and then taking his arm and leading him up to the table.

The conversation paused, and Kat tensed. *This is your chance! Come on! Speak!*

She opened her mouth just as Kýrios Zafirakis turned to her. His dark eyes drove into hers, sharp-tipped drills, then flicked away. Words died on her tongue, her cheeks going hot and cold, her cool-drink fantasy shattering to bits. The way he'd glared at her in that second: wishing she'd disappear—no, worse—wishing she'd never been there in the first place.

Someone touched her arm. "Katina?" Yeorgia. Asking her a question. Kat couldn't focus on her words. Why wouldn't Theofilus look at her?

"Theofilus." Kýrios Zafirakis waved his grandson toward Yeorgia.

Theofilus shot Kat a brief look, the color in his cheeks too high, too bright. Then he left with Yeorgia.

Kat whipped to Mom, whispering, "Um, where's Yeorgia going?"

"Boy, are you spacey," said Mom. "She told you she needed help bringing over more drinks. But don't worry, Theofilus is helping her."

She patted Kat's arm, then offered Kýrios Zafirakis a beer. With a gruff "*Efcharistó*," he nodded and followed Mom's motion to go up the steps to the early evening shade of the arbor-covered table.

The dinner was not going well. Squeezed on the bench between Manolis and Theíos Nick, Kat couldn't drink or eat, much less *move*, without rubbing against one or the other. She glanced to the far end of the table where Theofilus sat between Yeorgia and Mom.

How had this happened? One moment they all milled about the table, and the next Kyría Marula had nudged her in beside Manolis. She'd hoped Theofilus and Yeorgia would hurry back so that she could get him to sit with her. By the time they returned, Theofilus carrying a metal tub full of ice and sodas, Theíos Nick had already taken the spot. Trapped, Kat watched Yeorgia and Theofilus move around the table, offering drinks like a professional waiter team.

Then at the very moment she'd tried to catch Theofilus's eye, Kýrios Zafirakis called to him. Theofilus had looked at her—another hasty glimpse—but had turned away before she could tell what was in his eyes.

Now she was stuck. On her left, Theíos Nick talked to James and Nikos, lecturing to them about *várkes*. Even getting lost at sea couldn't curb their boat obsession. On her right,

Manolis leaned over his plate, breathing heavily while shoveling in tomato and feta salad. *Blech and double blech.* Kat stabbed her fork at the pile of *marithiá* on her plate. When the tiny fish scattered under the sharp tines, she copied James and Nikos, eating with her fingers.

She attempted to concentrate on the crunchy, lemony taste of the fish but couldn't keep from peeking at Theofilus. He sat on the edge of his seat, ready for flight, his fork moving machine-quick from plate to mouth. Was it unbearable for him, too? Being at this table, surrounded, like—like when she was at the beach and those jerks Michalis and Efthimios showed up?

She nibbled at her fish, her appetite shrinking with each passing moment. If only she could talk to him. But every time his eyes found hers, Kat had to look away, her very skin flinching at the thought that everyone—Kýrios Zafirakis most of all—could see whatever it was that buzzed between them.

All at once Theofilus put his fork down, pulled a small notebook and pen from his back pocket, and began to sketch, his expression going dreamy and far away.

So. That was it? A place inside Kat shriveled, leaving her dull, alone. She ripped her eyes away, landing them on Yeorgia.

Yeorgia.

How had Kat not noticed how pretty she was? Her hair rested on her shoulders, a length of shimmery satin, the thin band holding it away from her face matching her yellow dress. And her expression: calm and smooth. Now turning to give Kýrios Zafirakis a gentle smile.

Kat froze, fingers holding a tiny fish in midair. *Unbelievable!* Kýrios Zafirakis smiled back at Yeorgia, completely open and sunny.

Manolis nudged her arm. "Something is wrong?" he asked. "With the fish?"

"No," muttered Kat.

"Is hard for you. Everyone speaking Greek only. Is no good for you."

"Yeah." She dropped the fish back on her plate. "Whatever."

"I could teach you." He grinned when she faced him. "Greek words. A few phrases."

This guy gave new meaning to the word *dense*.

"After yesterday," she said, trying to ignore the oily crumb of feta clinging to his lip, "what makes you think I want to learn *anything* from you?"

Manolis's brow puckered.

"Oh, come on." She lowered her voice. "Hello? At the beach? All that stuff about 'American girls'?"

"I don't say anything about American girls."

Kat frowned. True, *he* actually hadn't.

Manolis continued. "And Michalis and Efthimios? They think you are older. Anyway, they are joking. Only joking."

For one instant Kat was back on the docks, her arms stinging as though Michalis and Efthimios grabbed at her again. *Some joke.*

"Those guys"—she had to work hard to keep her voice steady—"are totally lame."

"*Sýgnomi*, Kat. I am sorry for this. Yes, they are *vlákes*, eh, stupid boys."

If he only knew.

"But"—he went on, and though he didn't look at her now, his attention bent on scraping blue paint from under a fingernail, his voice deepened—"they tell me about last night. About you. Out by yourself."

"I-I went for a walk," she said, just as low. "I couldn't sleep."

Manolis cut her a look, his know-it-all snicker making the skin on the back of her neck prickle.

"Because of the *jet lag.*" She swallowed, not liking the sight of her reflection, small and pale, in his pupils. "And—and the heat. I went for a walk and those guys were—big surprise— totally stupid about that, too."

"Is okay. *I* understand."

What did he understand?

"Your mother and Kyría Sofia. They know about this? About your walk?"

"No," Kat murmured, "and I'm not going to do it again." She picked up her fork, taking her time spearing a piece of tomato. "It would be great if you kept it to yourself."

"Okay." That idiot *heh-heh* snicker again. "I like secrets."

His tone made Kat's shoulders want to twitch. Did he know about them leaving her with Theofilus, too?

A burst of laughter and loud talk pulled Kat's attention to the end of the table. Kýrios Zafirakis was lit up as if a flame burned inside him. Beer mug in hand, he beckoned toward Theofilus. Theofilus ripped out whatever he'd been drawing and stuffed the paper in his pocket, then handed Kýrios Zafirakis the notebook. Kýrios fanned through the pages, shaking his head with amusement. As he passed it back, he gestured first toward Yeorgia, who sat doll-like, eyes down and cheeks tinged with pink, and then to Theía Tassia and Mom. Both women chuckled away at whatever it was he was going on about in loud Greek.

Kat elbowed Manolis. "What's he saying?"

Manolis listened, then whispered, "He tell them Theofilus spend too much time drawing, eh, then he say nice things for Yeorgia. She look like his wife. As a little girl."

"That's creepy."

"Now he say, he know Yeorgia is a good Greek girl."

Kýrios Zafirakis reached behind Yeorgia to swat at Theofilus's shoulder, and Yeorgia looked up at Kat with big, miserable eyes. *Poor kid!* Kat offered her a little smile, but her lips dropped when Manolis half laughed, half snorted into her ear.

"He say there are very few good Greek girls left. And Theofilus need to get his nose out of his drawing and listen to his *pappoús*. Need to pay attention."

Still speaking, Kýrios Zafirakis peered around the table, but when he reached Kat, his gaze lingered as if he was talking directly to her. Talking to her as if she, not Theofilus, was the one who needed to pay attention.

Kat's eyes swept to Theofilus and held. His expression, a twisted mixture of agony and confusion, said everything. No matter who Kýrios Zafirakis's comments were for, Theofilus had heard him loud and clear.

CHAPTER TWENTY-SIX

hy was Kýrios Zafirakis so against her?
Kat stared down at her half-eaten dinner. Because she wasn't Greek? Was that why Theofilus acted hot and cold? Had his grandfather said something about her? Or maybe this dinner was making Theofilus realize how crazy last night was, being all alone with her American, totally-not-a-good-Greek-girl self.

Gah! She couldn't sit at this table for another second. Fingers trembling, Kat grabbed her plate and glass and stood, gesturing to Theíos Nick that she wanted out. As he shifted to let her go by, she jolted. *Wait a minute.* She *was* Greek. Half Greek, anyway.

A touch on her elbow had Kat looking down into Theíos Nick's confused face. Then the sudden quiet had her glancing around at the others, now silent and watching her. Barely able to breathe, she mumbled, "Excuse me," and hurried away from the table.

When she was alone in the kitchen, Kat stood clutching her dishes, her brain reeling. Was that why Mom was so desperate to spend the summer in Paralia? Did she actually think being here would magically wake up the Greek half in her kids? Like Greekness was some *team* they could join? A bark of unhappy laughter escaped through Kat's lips. *Yeah, sure.* If only she had her computer, then she could search up some "Top Tips for Being Greek."

Because she itched to throw her dishes against the wall, Kat forced herself to walk to the sink. She deposited her plate but held on to her glass. *Half Greek.* She sipped her water. What did that even mean?

She lowered the glass, something in her going hollow and achy. What if it meant nothing? What if *that* was the truth?

The glass slipped from her fingers, clattering in the sink as if it would break but only rolling against her plate, her undrunk water washing down the drain.

Yiayiá and Theía Tassia came into the kitchen then, each loaded down with plates and silverware. Yiayiá shooed Kat away from the sink, diving right into the cleanup dance with Tassia: one scraping food into the garbage and the other wrapping up leftovers, both talking competition-level fast.

Amused chatter drifted in from the patio. One thing for sure, Kat did *not* want to go back out there. Did not want to face any more babbling Greek voices.

She grabbed a freshly scraped plate and returned to the sink. She'd simply stay with Yiayiá in the kitchen, cleaning up until everyone—until Theofilus—went home.

"*Efcharistó,* Katina *mou,*" Yiayiá said, but shook her head, taking the plate from Kat's hands. "You go outside. With kids."

Exactly where Kat didn't want to be.

She edged toward the back door, but Tassia said, "Katina?" and, motioning toward the patio, put a plate filled with honey-drenched, papery-thin pastry triangles into Kat's hands.

Kat headed up the hall, pausing inside the doorway. The grown-ups lounged at the table, but there was no sign of any kids.

With a deep breath, she pushed through the wooden beads. "There you are," said Mom, reaching out for the dessert. "Yeorgia and the boys went to the other cottage to check out the repair job on the raft. Why don't you run over and join them?"

"Sure," Kat said, backing away, imagining her fake-smiling lips stretching and breaking. Around the side of the house, she slumped down on the swing.

She wouldn't follow the others. Wouldn't follow Theofilus. She saw his face again—fierce and then blank—and her chest squeezed as if it were being clenched in a steel fist. Images of being with him the night before rolled behind her eyes. He was probably being polite. Polite to a strange, foreign girl. *Except* . . . Her fingertips dug into the cushion. *What about his watercolor of her?*

The gate swung open and Yeorgia walked through followed by Theofilus.

"There you are!" Yeorgia hurried up the steps. "I think you will come, but, no."

Before Kat could say anything, Tassia's voice sang out from around the house. "Yeorgia!"

Yeorgia threw Kat a bright look and hurried away.

Kat sat motionless, aware only that she and Theofilus were alone. The swing rocked slightly when he sat. Instantly, the silence was unbearable. She turned, and his eyes were hot on hers.

"Kat," he whispered, "I—"

Quick footsteps interrupted. Yeorgia again, the plate of dripping golden triangles in her hand.

"Theofilus, *baklavás?*" said Yeorgia, offering up the plate.

Theofilus took a piece.

"Katina?"

"No. Thanks, though." Kat widened her eyes at Yeorgia, lifting her chin in what she hoped was the universal gesture of "please go now."

Yeorgia widened her own eyes. "Kýrios Zafirakis ask for Theofilus," she said, her voice quick and breathless. "I tell him we are *all* here." She turned to Theofilus, giving him the Greek version.

"Ah," said Theofilus.

"Oh," said Kat.

With an apologetic shrug, Yeorgia put the plate down on a nearby table, returning with a piece of *baklavás* cupped in her hand. Theofilus shifted close to Kat to make room for Yeorgia on the swing.

Kat listened to the two of them crunch into their dessert. The smell of the *baklavás* made the air sweet. She twisted her head the tiniest bit and caught Theofilus putting his last bite in his mouth. A small flake of pastry fell to his lower lip. Without even realizing she would, Kat lifted her hand. Before she touched him, reason returned and her finger detoured, pointing to his mouth.

"You've got . . ."

He stopped her words with the quickness of his smile. She watched him rub his thumb over his lip, then put it in his mouth.

The wanting came sharp and hot, and for a second Kat couldn't breathe, couldn't even understand exactly what it was she wanted.

Theofilus smiled at her again, this time in that slow way, and she knew her thoughts were as clear to him as if they were painted on her forehead.

Loud talk and the gate banging open brought James and Nikos into the yard. Manolis, a step behind, closed the gate after them.

Yeorgia called out about the *baklavás* and all three bounded up the steps. James and Nikos took a piece in each hand, stuffing their faces before bolting off. Manolis picked up a piece, then dragged one of the patio chairs close to the swing.

About to take a bite, Manolis paused, looking at Kat. "You try this? *Baklavás?*"

"I'm pretty stuffed," she said. "Maybe later."

"Yeorgia make this," he said, his mouth full now. "Is very smart for girls to learn cooking." His tone—pompous beyond belief—strangely mimicked Kýrios Zafirakis's. "Yeorgia know this is how good Greek girls get husbands."

Kat looked at Yeorgia. Why didn't she drill the jerk? Yeorgia shrugged as if she'd heard Manolis's words a thousand times.

Kat turned back to Manolis. "You're joking, right?"

"No. Why I am joking?"

"Because—because why should Yeorgia even be thinking about 'getting a husband'? She's only twelve. Besides, she wants to be a—"

"Katina?" Yeorgia reached across Theofilus fast and gripped Kat's arm. "I teach you *baklavás?* Okay?"

Don't. Yeorgia's expression insisted—*don't tell him about the pilot thing.*

"Yeah, uh, that'd be great." Kat swung back to Manolis. "But because *I* want to learn, not because I want to impress a guy."

Manolis's answering smirk made Kat want to smack him.

Theofilus spoke, bursting the moment.

"What did he say?" said Kat.

"He say—" Their words overlapping, Yeorgia and Manolis

both paused, cracking up. Yeorgia continued. "Theofilus say he wish he can speak English."

"Why don't you?" Kat said, looking from Theofilus to Yeorgia. "I mean, you guys do, sort of. So why doesn't he?"

As if he'd understood her, Theofilus began to answer, but Manolis cut him off with a loud snort.

"What?" said Kat.

"He choose *Italian*," Manolis said, snickering away.

"Manolis!" Yeorgia's voice held a firm note Kat hadn't heard from her before. "Theofilus say he choose Italian," she went on, softer now. "Because, eh, next year he want to go to Italía. For school."

To Italy? For school?

"This why he is here," Yeorgia said, "fishing with his *pappoús*. He earn money to go for a school in Florence. He want to study there. To be . . . *Éla* Manolis, tell Katina what is *kallitéchnis*."

"Artist," said Manolis.

An artist. Kat smiled up at Theofilus. Of course.

The way Theofilus watched her, eyes half closed, told Kat that he was thinking of their time together the night before as well.

They both stopped smiling when Manolis scoffed again, giving Theofilus an earful, before continuing to rant in English.

"Artist is not job. No money. Fishing is good business. *Éla*, Theofilus."

The more Manolis said, the stonier Theofilus's expression grew, making Kat wish she could think of anything to shut Manolis up. But what could she say? That she'd looked through a big book of Theofilus's art? One that included a watercolor of her? That he was a genius? How would she explain that?

She gripped the seat cushion on either side of her thighs, her fingers under the edges of her skirt. An instant later a finger—Theofilus's finger—touched her pinkie. She went still, aware of Manolis talking on and on but with no idea of anything he actually said. Everything was Theofilus, his finger wrapping around hers.

"Why you smiling, Kat?" Manolis's gaze fastened on her. "What is funny?"

Theofilus's finger squeezed hers, and she cleared her throat, turning her giggle to a cough. "Nothing. Nothing's funny. Anyway, who cares if artists don't make a lot of money?"

"Money is very important," murmured Yeorgia, "a job is very important."

"You Americans are babies," said Manolis, trying to sound all jokey. "In TV, movies, online, you go where you want. Do what you want. This is not Greece. Here, our family tells us what we must do. To keep the family strong. Keep Greece strong."

Now Manolis spoke Greek again, his words a flattening bulldozer, making Yeorgia blink as if about to cry and Theofilus stare down at his lap.

Kat pressed her finger against Theofilus's. When he looked at her, a light had gone out of him.

"He can't tell you this, but I tell you," Manolis continued. "This is why Kýrios Zafirakis does not like Americans."

Kat jolted. "What are you even talking about?"

"Before. I hear him talking to Kyría Sofia and Kyría Maria. He tell them about his son. Not this one's father." Manolis waved a hand at Theofilus. "But his older boy. How he love America, go to university in America. He meet an American girl and get married, and now? Now they have children, but they don't speak Greek. Don't come to Greece. He says 'is no good.'"

Kat watched Manolis, both mesmerized and repulsed by how gossiping made his face glow. Then what he actually said sank in. *Married American. Kids didn't speak Greek. Never came to Greece.* She swallowed once, dryness making her throat stick. Exactly what Mom had done.

CHAPTER TWENTY-SEVEN

hairs scraping and voices approaching cut Manolis short. He and Yeorgia rose, and Kat whirled to Theofilus. She opened her mouth, wanting to say something, but what? A second later, the grown-ups descended. Theofilus let go of her finger and jammed his hand into his pocket, plucking something out. Quickly, he stuffed whatever it was under the side of her skirt where moments before their hands had been linked. Then he stood and walked to where his grandfather thanked Yiayiá and Mom with a loud, hearty "*Efcharistó.*"

Kat fished under her skirt, finding a folded bit of paper. No one was looking, so she brought the paper onto her lap.

He'd given her a rough sketch of his fishing boat. Her head shot up. This was what he'd been drawing at the table.

Like he could feel her eyes, Theofilus pivoted. She touched the paper, and he moved his hand slightly, pointing up. He dropped his fingers as his grandfather draped an arm around him.

What was he trying to tell her? Kat tucked the paper in her pocket and tilted her head up. The moon, huge but not nearly full, glowed above.

The boat? The moon? Her heart skittering in her chest, Kat rose from the swing and moved next to Mom, who was now in the thick of another conversation with Kýrios Zafirakis.

Kat kept her face blank, polite, then let her eyes drift to Theofilus. He mouthed a single word.

What? She gave her head the ghost of a shake. He mouthed the word again, "*Apópse,*" and intensified his gaze.

She nodded. Whatever *apópse* meant, she'd find out.

With a loud and final "*Kalinýchta,*" Kýrios Zafirakis propelled Theofilus down Yiayiá's steps, and he was gone. Gone.

Kat barely felt the pressure when Mom put her hand on the back of her neck.

"Well, well," Mom said, "*that* was interesting."

"What do you mean?"

"Oh, nothing. It's just been a long time since I met a man that set in his ways." Mom let out a breathy chuckle. "I'm pretty sure my father was the last one."

Kat frowned, inwardly filing what Mom said for later. Right now, she had a mystery to solve.

"Mom?"

"Hmm?"

Kat clutched the drawing of the boat in her pocket. "What does *apópse* mean?"

"*Apópse?* 'Tonight.'"

CHAPTER TWENTY-EIGHT

ive minutes into her run, Kat's chest was a burning cramp, and she couldn't catch her breath. *Stop! You started too fast.* She slowed almost to a walk, gulping air. Even as the scent of pine and salt soothed the stingy fizz behind her breastbone, the expanse of late night wrapped around her, a suffocating blanket. She was nuts. *Nuts.* After what had happened on the docks with Michalis and Efthimios, what was she *doing* out here?

Of course, the *tavérna* was long closed—she'd made *sure* to find out about that—but part of her couldn't believe she'd snuck out again to run alone in the dark.

Yet here she was. And she would keep sneaking out because—because she *had* to run, and this was the only way.

Besides, she wasn't really alone. Now there was Theofilus. Kat's breathing settled, and her stride went from choppy and robotic to long and fluid. Theofilus and his invitation.

She moved faster, testing the feel of her limbs. Little by little, she increased her speed. *Love. The. Running.* She smiled and pushed herself to run faster, wanting to touch the invisible boundary of what her body could do. Wanting to reach that line and leap past it.

She shifted the flashlight from one hand to the other. It hadn't helped her much with those idiot—no, *vlákes*—boys

Michalis and Efthimios, but the weight of it was almost friendly. As if looking for more friends, Kat hunted the landscape. There was the moon above, gleaming and silvery pale. And below, the shadowy edge of the shore and the sea beyond. How the water glittered, a wash of black sequin-covered satin. The tightness in her chest loosened, and her fear slipped away. No one needed to be out this late, and if a car or a motorbike did appear, she'd see their light first and disappear into the dark.

She ran on, her brain clearing and her body humming. Everything faded except the road under her pounding shoes and the twinkle of a couple of tiny lights marking Paralia ahead.

She picked out the jetty and then the docks, and the desire to see Theofilus zigzagged through her, an insistent wave. She slowed.

No. She sped up again, streaking by the docks, almost holding her breath. She couldn't stop now. Losing that need to keep running—even for a second—hurt, a physical pain. Of course, she wanted to see Theofilus, pretty much more than anything, but she couldn't change her running plan. She wouldn't be one of those girls who gave up plans, important plans, the minute there was a boy.

What about Mike Doherty?

Amusement hitched her breath a little. All that crushing on his photograph seemed so far away, as if it had happened to another girl. Mike Doherty had nothing to do with her or what running had come to mean to her. Sure, she wanted to be on the cross-country team and be friends with her teammates, but no matter what else happened in the fall, one thing was simple. She would run. It had become a need, like food or water. A need deep inside her.

Half Greek.

Her amusement evaporated. Need or not, *that* was inside her, too.

Don't think about it. Think about the running. Only the running.

She pushed on, past the dark *tavérna*, past the market, past everything Paralia. The second she started up the mountain road, the scorched dry of night melted to heated syrup. Her breath shortened, the back of her throat closing, her lungs straining. She climbed on, higher and higher. Then a switch flipped and her lungs and legs shut down, both as used up as squeezed-out tubes of toothpaste.

Trembling, she stopped, hands on her hips and slightly bent over. When her chest quit threatening to explode, she straightened. The night was too dark to make out the top of the mountain road, but like a living presence, she knew it was there, waiting for her.

Like Theofilus.

She ran her tongue over her dry lips, already tasting the *lemonáda* he would offer her. Besides the salt and dryness of exertion, she discovered a new taste. Warm and electric.

Yes. She would go to him now.

CHAPTER TWENTY-NINE

Prickly energy pulsed through Kat, making her walk fast through the shadows of the sleeping town. Way out by the stone jetty, small guide lights winked over the water. At the docks, the boats loomed, inviting and mysterious, everything dark except for the dim gleam coming from the lower portholes of one now-familiar boat.

Tendrils of hair tickled across her sweaty forehead, and as she scraped them away, her steps lost momentum. She looked down and plucked the damp, clinging fabric of her running tank away from her belly. *Yuck!* Here she was meeting Theofilus, and she was the grunge-beast-of-life.

Scrubbing a palm over her face, she walked on. Next time—her breath caught as her brain leapt from this night into the possibility of future nights—she'd figure out how to clean up before meeting him.

She stepped down onto the docks, then tilted her head back. The moon, circled by pinprick stars, wheeled in the sky, appearing to move simultaneously closer and farther away. She pressed a hand to her chest. *Jeez! Chill already.* Everything in her careened in too many directions, though, as if she'd dropped a bag of marbles on a slippery floor, and even watching them scatter, she couldn't see where they all went.

Was that it? Did she want to be able to see all the marbles, know where they were all going?

On the boat now, she tiptoed to the door leading below. It was slightly ajar. She pushed it open, wanting to call to Theofilus. Instead, she eased down the stairs, quiet ringing in her ears. Was he even here? Kýrios Zafirakis's leathery scowl flashed behind her eyes; with a shiver, she shrugged it away.

Then she was in the cabin, the lantern inside glazing everything with a warm spill of low amber light. And there— stretched out on the bench—Theofilus, asleep.

He lay on top of his sleeping bag, his expression still and smooth, one of those painted angels. Or maybe a character from a long-ago fairy tale. *Sleeping Beauty.* Kat moved toward him, laughing soundlessly at the idea of herself in the role of kissing prince, her pulse skipping at the thought of actually putting her mouth on his.

On his pillow, a pair of glasses sat open and askew. Next to them perched a sketchpad with a pencil stuck in the spiral binding and a small blue book. She leaned over to see the book, and her braid swung down, sweeping across his shoulder.

With a startled shudder, he jerked up. *"Ti káneis?"*

Kat wrenched away, but his shoulder banged into her chin, and she let out a strangled cry, stumbling back.

Both breathing hard, they stared at each other.

"Ach . . ." Theofilus's whisper broke the spell. His fingers came to her chin, and his touch made everything in her move too fast again.

"I'm fine," she said, drawing away. "I-I didn't mean to scare you. I—" She broke off, made herself take a slowing-down breath. "I didn't mean to scare you," she repeated, pointing at him. "Sorry." She put her hands together, leaning her cheek on them as if asleep, and then pouted her lips into an apologetic face. *This was so lame.*

Theofilus sat up taller, rubbing his eyes and clearing his throat. He didn't say anything, only gestured to the cooler.

"*Naí.*" She hesitated—*okay, she could do this.* "*Thélo. Lemonáda. Parakaló.*"

Theofilus gave her a quick grin and went for the drinks. As they both took long swigs, he sat back down on the sleep bench.

"*Éla,*" he said, patting the place beside his leg.

She sat, her movements careful as if she were afraid of breaking something. Their shoulders were close but didn't touch, the few empty inches between them rippling, the very air pulling and pushing, nearly breathing. Moments ticked, the only noises the creaking of the boat and the hollow bottle sound of them sipping their drinks.

Out of the corner of her eye, Kat could see the frayed hem of Theofilus's shorts resting on his knees, the shadowy fuzz of hair on his shins. She glanced down at her own legs, and her running shorts seemed impossibly short, her thighs pale and pinkish. She brought her knees up, but stopped before the dusty bottoms of her running shoes touched the sleeping bag. Reaching to take off the shoes, she stopped again, her face flooding with heat. *Nasty!* How could she even *think* of taking off her shoes?

When Theofilus touched her arm, she jumped. He pointed to her shoes and to the sleeping bag.

"Is . . . okay," he said, a blush spreading across his cheeks.

Kat nodded and tucked up her legs.

Theofilus tapped her shoe, his brow crinkling. "*Yiatí?*" He bent his arms at the elbows and pumped them.

Why was she running? She let out a small laugh. That was the same question she'd asked herself while she ran.

"I . . . God." She pointed to her mouth, shaking her head, and he raised a finger, asking her to wait, then reached for the blue book, and held it out to her.

English-Greek Dictionary. Wow. Sparks of pleasure ran through her while she flipped to the English part.

"*Omáda*," she said, a finger under the word for "team."

"*Kalós*," murmured Theofilus, shifting closer, his whole side pressing against hers now. The contact sent tickling-ribbon thrills across every bit of her. He gave her a swift look and took the dictionary, bending his head as he leafed through. He pointed to a word.

"*Scholeío*," she pronounced. "Yeah. For 'school.'" *That* word was close enough to English. She could remember that one. "*Scholeío omáda.*"

Mumbling in Greek, he turned more pages, then said, "You fast?"

Kat made a scoffing sound, shook her head. "Not really," she said, but hesitated. *Why not tell the truth?* "*Naí.* I am." She read over his finger again. "*Grígora.*"

He laughed, short and whispery, and her cheeks burned as she realized what else her words suggested. His eyes fell to her mouth, and her insides did a long, slow twist, everything in her wanting to lean closer—

All at once Theofilus was on his feet. Kat blinked up at him. She hadn't actually *leaned.* Had she?

He gestured toward the galley, then shook his head as if annoyed with himself, and went behind the counter. Crouching out of sight, he opened one of the lower cupboards, the noises he made fast and shoving.

Was he angry? Kat took quick sips of her drink, the lemony soda burning her tongue.

When Theofilus straightened, between his tight mouth and the way he gripped whatever was in his hands—as if he didn't know what to do with it—a light bulb went on in her head.

He was nervous, too, *maybe even more than her.*

He held out what Kat could now see was a portable radio, and she laughed her relief.

"Music? Yeah, good idea," she said, "let's listen to music."

He sat again, not so close to her this time, and turned on the radio, all his attention focused on adjusting the blare of the volume, twisting the tuning button. Loud hip-hop blasted.

"All right!" Kat's insides warmed, as if she'd unexpectedly run into a long-lost best friend.

"I like," he said, passing the radio to her, his face happy and relaxed.

Kat beamed. This is what she'd be doing at home in New Canaan. Hanging out with a friend, probably Angie, listening to tunes.

She glanced behind Theofilus and grabbed his sketchpad. "Show me?" she said, patting the pad, then her chest.

"This," he said, tapping the closed sketchbook and shaking his head. "No finish."

Kat cocked her head in a plea, and with a windy sigh, he took the sketchpad from her and opened it.

Bunches of small, penciled drawings covered each page, some of the images crude, others fully detailed like black-and-white snapshots. Kat studied the bits and pieces. Where had he seen these things, these people?

She pointed to an image of two clasped hands. "*Yiatí . . . óchi állos?*" *Why no more?*

"This," he said, running his finger from the drawing of hands to a couple of the others, "lígo. Little." He tapped the side of his head, rifling pages in the dictionary again.

Kat read the word he indicated aloud. "Thymámai. 'Remember.'"

His smile asked if she understood.

And she did. These sketches were just that: quick memories, notes jotted down. And wasn't it funny how thymámai was like both the English and Greek words for "thyme"—the sweet, minty herb that had reminded her of Theofilus earlier and that she smelled a trace of in the cabin right now.

He turned to the next page, and Kat pulled back. Sketches of gnarled hands, a hooked nose, tight mouth, sharp eyes: each a bit of Kýrios Zafirakis.

Even though the quiet buzz of happy-sounding music filled the cabin, the air stilled, all energy sucked away.

"Your pappoús?" Kat said, her voice barely a whisper.

Without taking his eyes off the page, Theofilus nodded.

"Your pappoús likes . . . ? Wait." She fumbled for the dictionary again, found the word for 'art.' "Téchni?"

He shook his head. "Pappoús like Manolis."

Likes Manolis?

Kat frowned, and then she remembered the conversation on Yiayiá's swing. She put her hand on his arm.

"You. Understand?" he said, eyes fierce now.

"Yeah, I understand," she murmured, "no money in art. I mean—in téchni, no drachmí."

Theofilus's face dissolved into an amused grin, and Kat wanted to laugh with him, but there was more she needed to understand.

"Theofilus?"

She looked down at her fingers, where they still rested on the fine gold-tipped hairs of his forearm, then made herself look at him even though his eyes on hers were intense enough that she wondered if this was how staring at the sun would feel.

"Your *pappoús* no like . . ." She put a hand on her chest. "Me?"

Theofilus blew out a long breath and closed his eyes. When he opened them, Kat's insides fell. She didn't need words to tell her the answer, but the words he didn't say scraped at her.

"Why?" she blurted. "I mean, I know *why*. But everyone else knows how bad I feel about what happened with James and Nikos. And *so what* if I'm only half Greek? Why won't he at least give me a chance?"

Theofilus watched her, his expression wretched enough that she knew he had to have gotten her drift.

"Pappoús." He glanced around the cabin, then took the dictionary, but didn't open it. "Pappoús no like America . . . *ach!*"

He threw open the dictionary, almost ripping the pages. "Afraid," he said, holding up the book to Kat.

"*Fovisménos*," she read, almost smiling again at recognizing a part of an English word in the Greek. "He's afraid of me? He's got Kat-a-phobia?"

Theofilus cracked up, nodding as he picked up his sketchbook. Hurriedly, he found a fresh page and drew with quick sharp strokes.

On one side of the page, he sketched sticklike figures of the fishing boat with his *pappoús* on the deck. Pappoús did not look happy. Up in the air, he drew a stick Theofilus sitting on an airplane flying over the ocean. On the opposite side, he outlined the good old U. S. of A., then penciled in a stick girl with a braid and big running shoes standing in the middle.

"You've *got* to be joking," said Kat.

She thumbed through the dictionary again, but didn't find "joking." She tried "kidding," and her tongue tripped over the tough combination of vowels. "*Koroïdia.*"

"No," said Theofilus, his smile now mischievous. "No *koroïdia.*"

So, what Manolis said was true. Kýrios Zafirakis saw her as a threat to the Greekness of his family. That was nuts. The whole situation would have been hysterically funny if it wasn't clear that he could make it impossible for her to see Theofilus—or worse, that maybe he would punish Theofilus.

"I should go," she said.

Theofilus clicked his tongue and, like the night before, put his hand on her shoulder. "*Óchi*, no now." He lowered his eyes, his lashes grazing the tops of his cheekbones. "I want you *edó*, here."

Kat swallowed hard, a little afraid of how happy what he'd said made her. Seeing him this way was crazy. But she wanted to be with him. Wanted the chance to get to know him; to understand how he felt about his art, about his family, about school even.

There was more, too. She wanted him to understand her. How she felt about . . . she didn't know exactly what. Maybe everything.

Walking home, Theofilus held her hand. When they reached the bottom of Yiayiá's lane, they stopped at the same time. Kat glanced down at their joined hands, not wanting to be the one to break the contact.

"Good night," Theofilus whispered, his accent making the words new and sweet.

"Yeah." Her voice trailed off, that breathless moment coming again.

Theofilus didn't smile, or move away, and Kat didn't know if she moved or he did, but all at once their mouths touched, quick and gentle.

When he lifted his head, he whispered again, "Good night."

"*Kalinýchta*," she whispered back.

"*Ávrio*," he said, giving her hand a light squeeze.

She nodded and watched him disappear into the darkness. Brushed her finger over her kissed lips.

Yes, to ávrio. Whatever that meant. Yesyesyes.

CHAPTER THIRTY

When Kat peeked out her window the next morning, Mom, Theía Tassia, and Yeorgia chattered away on the patio, all of them dressed for the beach. For a second, observing them busily stuffing towels into bags, Kat had the sensation of being in a dimension apart. A dimension where life at Yiayiá's went on as usual, while she traveled alongside in her secret, freshly kissed, nighttime-running world.

"There's my sleepyhead," said Mom, spotting her. "The boys will be here in a minute. If you hurry and get ready, you can come to the beach with us."

"Okay."

Kat moved away from the window and was about to strip off her sleep shirt, when a light knocking sounded outside her doorway.

"Katina?" Yeorgia poked in her head. "*Sýgnomi*, sorry. You are dressing." She started to duck out.

"No, Yeorgia, it's fine. What is it?"

"I . . ." Yeorgia lowered her voice as she came into the room. "I don't get to talk to you last night. Kýrios Zafirakis say—say too much things about Greek girls. You are not mad with me? About Theofilus?"

Theofilus. Kat dropped the tiny smile creeping across her face. "Mad? No, I'm not mad."

"But. You and Theofilus—"

"What about Theofilus?" It was Mom, right in the doorway.

"Nothing," said Kat quickly. "We were—we were saying he seemed nice."

"Yes. He was nice." Mom grinned, looking right at Kat, then let her gaze wander around the room. "Too bad his *pappoús* was such a grump."

Kat followed her mother's traveling eyes and itched to kick the jumble of clothes and gear out of sight. *Jeez!* If Mom noticed her connection with Theofilus last night, what else would she notice?

Stretching a foot to nudge her running shoes under the bed, Kat froze as Mom's attention came back to her.

"Did you sleep all right, sweets? You look tired."

"I-I am tired. Yeah. I think I woke up a bunch of times. Probably from the jet lag or I don't know."

"Hmm, James and I are pretty much over that. But I guess everyone's different. *Éla*, Yeorgia." Mom squeezed Yeorgia's shoulder. "Let's let Kat get dressed and maybe pick up her room."

When they were out the door, Kat shoved her running shoes out of sight and zipped her sweaty running clothes safely away in a suitcase pocket. *Whew!* She hauled up the *tagári* from the floor and ran a finger down the Artemis figure. "I know, I know," she muttered, "be more careful."

By the time she was ready and out on the patio, James and Nikos were coming through the gate, lugging none other than the yellow raft.

"Are you kidding me?" She rolled her eyes at Mom. "Are you actually letting them use that again?"

"Those two love that raft. And I think with four of us there, they should be fine." Mom turned. "Good. Here comes Yiayiá with the snacks."

Yiayiá handed Mom a cooler, then marched over to James and Nikos. She put a hand on each of their shoulders, murmuring in a gentle tone. A second later she shifted to her *chop-chop* bark and, after giving each boy a quick cuff on the side of the head, grabbed them close, hugging their faces into her ample chest.

"Ah, yes," said Mom. "I think James and Nikos are going to be extra careful today. The wrath of Yiayiá is a strong motivator."

Moments later, they set off: Mom and Tassia in the lead, then James and Nikos with raft in tow, and Kat and Yeorgia bringing up the rear.

As the group reached the end of Yiayiá's lane, heat stung Kat's cheeks. There—right there—was where Theofilus kissed her. A scalding line traced from her belly down, and she let out a long breath.

"Katina?" Yeorgia's voice snapped her back to reality. "Something is wrong?"

"What?"

"You are sounding sad."

"No, I'm not sad." It was like when they were on the swing the day before. She wanted to talk to Yeorgia—*but*. "I-I wish I could have made a better impression on Kýrios Zafirakis last night."

They gave each other an *oh, well* look.

"It's okay," Kat went on, "it's not like he was going to give me much of a chance. He made it pretty obvious he doesn't want Theofilus to spend time with any Americans." She let her sentence fizzle, the weight of her secret making even the truth feel like a lie.

As they turned out of Yiayiá's lane, Yeorgia said, "Maybe you try another way. Make some *baklavás*? Maybe take it to his house."

"His house?"

"Kýrios Zafirakis live—there." Yeorgia pointed down another lane. "The house with, eh, you see this big fish on top. The one, it is metal?"

Kat squinted far down the lane. A fish-shaped copper weathervane perched on the roof of the pocket-sized house at the very end.

Kýrios Zafirakis lived right down there? In that mini-house? No wonder Theofilus had to stay on the boat. *Whoa!* That meant both nights when she and Theofilus were—

His final word to her from the night before buzzed into her head.

"Yeorgia? What does *ávrio* mean?"

"*Ávrio*? This mean 'tomorrow.'"

Tomorrow! Which meant today. Which meant—

A distant revving startled her. A motorbike engine.

The motorized whir grew, zinging along the back of Kat's neck, into her ears like a furious bee. She looked over her shoulder. Sure enough, a motorbike and rider whizzed down the hill.

Was it—? No. Not Helmet-Man. This rider didn't even wear a helmet, and his bike was bright blue, not all chipped and beaten up.

Kat wilted as she turned forward. Most of her would never choose to see Helmet-Jerk again, but a bit of her would've liked to have run into him one more time, like this, in broad daylight, surrounded by people.

The bike came closer, and the engine shut off. Kat glanced back. *Seriously?* It was Manolis.

"Good morning," he said all cheery, now coasting silently beside them.

Both Kat and Yeorgia said, "*Yassou,*" then Yeorgia smiled at the bike.

"What you do, Manolis? Your bike look—"

"Katina?" Manolis interrupted. "You like motorbikes? You want to ride with me?"

"No! I mean, thanks. But no."

His face clouded. "Maybe you like to go *fishing* instead?"

Did *everyone* notice something between her and Theofilus last night?

"No," she said fast. "I'm okay walking, and my mom wouldn't let me go on a motorbike anyway, you know, without a helmet."

"Yes," said Yeorgia, "where is your *krános?* Kyría Marula—"

"*Éla,* Yeorgia! I am talking to Katina."

Kat raised her eyebrows at Yeorgia, but Yeorgia only shrugged.

"Katina?" Manolis tapped her arm, his voice shifting from sour to sweet again. "Eh, maybe I find a helmet, and we go later. Okay?"

"Maybe," Kat said. She tried to smile, but her lips wouldn't cooperate.

"Good. Is settled. I see you at the beach."

His smug, full-of-expectation expression made her remember their conversation at the table the night before. Especially the part about how he liked secrets. *Wait.* Her insides jolted. Maybe his crack about fishing meant that he did know about Michalis and Efthimios leaving her with Theofilus that night.

She watched him zoom down the hill, and Yeorgia said, "Manolis like you. He want to impress you."

"I don't know. I think he wants to show off, you know, 'Look at me with the American girl.'" As the words came out of Kat's mouth, her star-of-the-cross-country-team-Mike fantasy popped into her head. *No, no, no.* What she'd wanted with the team, with Mike, was totally different. She wound the end of her braid around a finger. *Totally.*

Yeorgia interrupted Kat's thoughts. "Perhaps you are right. Last year, Manolis was *polý mikró.* Very small. We are at the beach, and boys tease him, say, 'Look, *nýo nyo.*'"

"What is a *nýo nyo?*"

"*Nýo nyo* is a man who is not a man. Like a man who is a baby." Yeorgia made a scared face, and they both cracked up. "Now, Manolis get big. I think he want to be a big man. This is why I ask you about cooking *baklavás* last night. When you want to talk about me and pilot."

"What?"

"Manolis think he is big man. That girls are for cooking. For cleaning. I don't want Manolis to say, 'Kyría Tassia. Yeorgia want to be a pilot.' Mamá and Babás want me to work in their shop. Maybe Mamá hear this about the pilot. Maybe she not like."

"So, you wanting to be a pilot is a secret?"

"No." Yeorgia clicked her tongue. "Is not a secret, but is for *me* to say. Not for Manolis, big man to make a joke. Big man who ride a motorbike with no *krános.*"

At Kat's confused expression, Yeorgia pointed to her head. "*Krános.* For motorbike."

"Right, helmet." Kat shook her head. "What's with riding motorbikes in this country anyway? Why doesn't everyone wear a—a *krános?*"

"Is not the law," said Yeorgia, "but Kyría Marula, if she see Manolis on this motorbike with no helmet? *Po po po!* She is very mad."

An image of Marula getting mad at Manolis over the helmet thing—maybe forbidding him to ride it—filled Kat's head. No way would she ride with him, but how perfect if Marula was the one who said no instead of her?

On the beach at last, Kat glanced over to Mom and Tassia setting up the umbrella. Nearby, Manolis's motorbike leaned on its kickstand, and he sprawled on his towel spread-eagle and already slick with tanning oil that reeked of too-sweet coconut. She wrinkled her nose. At least he didn't have on the totally gross teeny black bathing suit.

"Katina?" Yeorgia called to her from where she and the boys already waded into the water with the raft.

Kat hurried after them, and the cold, salty sea against her skin was as delicious as the biggest gulp of an icy drink. This was what being with Theofilus was like. Sparkly and electric; hot, hot skin plunging into cool, silky water. She dove deep and grinned, imagining him diving off his boat into this same water.

When she came up, her head bounced against inflated rubber.

"Hey," James said, leaning over the side of the raft. "Get in."

"I'm not sure I trust that thing," she said, splashing him.

"C'mon, it's totally cool."

Kat reached to hoist herself up, but hands from behind

grabbed her tight around the waist, thrusting her high. Moving too fast, she slid into the bottom of the raft, a floppy fish. She twisted just as Manolis hauled himself in after her. She rolled sideways, but the bottom of the raft, a too-mushy suction cup, held her, and he landed mostly on top of her.

She struggled against him as he attempted to lift himself off, but—but *was he?* His hands, elbows, legs were everywhere at once. Yeorgia cried out and James and Nikos yelled, the rubber of the raft making a squealing noise as bodies scrambled. A hard jab of her elbow to Manolis's ribs released her from what felt like the slimy grip of an octopus.

"What do you think you're doing?" she said, stumbling to sit on the raft's side.

"What is wrong?" Manolis sat up slowly. "I try to help you, but I slip."

He let out a weak chuckle, and she got a speck of pleasure when he rubbed the place where she elbowed him.

Yeorgia sat next to her, eyes huge. "You okay?"

Kat nodded, taking shallow breaths, working to erase Manolis's touch.

Manolis perched near, smiling at her, bland and innocent. As he turned away, however, his lips pursed the tiniest bit. The tiniest, self-satisfied bit.

Before knowing she would, Kat shoved him hard, tumbling him backward off the raft.

When he surfaced, sputtering and coughing, his cheeks blazed a deep, angry red.

"Katina? Why you do that?"

"Sorry. *I* slipped."

His mouth stretched into a hungry grin. "We play a game?"

"Aah, *no*," said Kat. Would this guy ever take a hint? Or

maybe that was the problem. Maybe he thought knowing her secret and keeping it meant he didn't *have* to take a hint.

At that moment, she had no interest in finding out. As he grabbed onto the raft, she dove off the other side. Kicking fast, she swam for the beach.

CHAPTER THIRTY-ONE

K at spent the rest of the day making sure never to be alone with Manolis. He seemed to be everywhere she was, though, coming back with them from the beach, staying for lunch, and then even hanging around to play cards with the boys during the *siesta*.

Yiayiá ran solid interference, insisting Kat help make the lunch and then shooing Manolis out of the kitchen when he offered to help. At least at the *siesta*, Kat could escape to her room. Her longed-for nap didn't happen, however; his voice out on the patio had the same effect as a mosquito buzzing in her ear.

When bedtime came, she was exhausted. As hard as she tried to stay up waiting for Paralia to shut down, she fell asleep.

The hour was way past late when she startled awake, rumpled and hanging halfway off her bed. A part of her considered skipping her run, wanting to rush straight to Theofilus, but no. She was a runner and she had to run.

"Okay, Artemis," she said under her breath as she jammed her bathing suit, a spare T-shirt, a brush, and a small towel into the *tagári*. "If any *vláka* idiots come up behind me, feel free to fire away with those arrows."

Tying the *tagári* tight across her back, she hefted her flashlight and headed out into her dark running world.

By the time she reached the mountain road, she cruised at top speed, her pace a steady, crunching *whumpf, whumpf, whumpf*. Beginning her ascent, she tracked the now-familiar shapes of the shadowed rocks and bushes she'd passed on previous nights. *The night*. It was her friend now, making her more in *lovelovelove* with the running than ever. *Opa!* She wanted to shout it to the midnight sky.

Smells and noises disappeared, unable to cut through the heat of exertion blazing across her cheeks and forehead. Except for her breath. Coming in scissoring puffs, each breath in and out roared furnace-loud in her ears, spurring her on. Just a little farther. A little farther. There. The tall bush standing by itself, its spiky leaves in stark relief against the starry midnight sky. That's where she'd stopped the night before.

She ran by the bush, propelling herself to keep going, keep going. Even when her body screamed for her to quit, she went on until the bulk of a roadside boulder offered up a landmark she'd be able to recognize the next time.

Legs all but boneless, she stopped. More quickly than she expected, they recovered. Her lungs burned, as scratchy as if she'd inhaled dust, but that sensation, too, wasn't as harsh and suffocating as it had been the night before.

She tipped her head back, grinning big. "I'm doing it," she whispered to the moon, the stars, "I'm getting there."

She longed for her water bottle, but running with it would make the *tagári* too heavy. Anyway, Theofilus would have drinks.

Theofilus.

She'd planned to take a dip in the sea, clean up before seeing Theofilus, but—asleep or awake—he had to have been waiting for her for hours.

She beamed. *Waiting for her.*

The next thing she knew she was on his boat, grabbing the cabin's door handle.

With a creaking rush, the door swung in. She stumbled, and Theofilus caught her.

"Katina?" He kept talking as he took her hand, the way he looked her over telling her he'd worried.

"I'm fine. I got a late start," she said, giddy, happy. "I . . ." She put her palms together, leaning her cheek against them to mime sleep.

He ran a hand through his hair, shaking his head, laughing, but not like he found anything funny. He waved toward the galley, going on in fast Greek.

That's when she spotted two empty soda bottles on the counter and, next to them, two of Theofilus's sketchpads, sitting open. Open as if people had been looking through them. And recently.

Her smile fading, Kat stepped to the counter and fingered one of the pads. "What's going on?" Her gaze shot to Theofilus. "Was—was someone *here?*"

He nodded, one quick up and down. "Michalis *kai* Efthimios."

The names tumbled from his lips. He spoke more, but Kat didn't even try to understand, hating the sizzle of shock geysering up from her belly to her throat. No *wonder* he'd worried. He probably thought they'd waylaid her. *God!* What if she'd burst into the cabin when they'd been there? She shuddered hard, watching Theofilus collect their empties, her vision blurring as if she were staring into a glaring-bright light. Because those boys *had* been there. *Right there, in the cabin!*

Then Theofilus was offering her a dripping-cold bottle.

She took the drink, forcing a smile, but couldn't shake the unhappy fog clouding her mind. "What—what did they want?" she said. "Michalis, Efthimios."

Theofilus's shoulders lifted and fell with a quick disinterested drop, but one side of his mouth curled down as if tasting food he didn't like.

"They want me," he said, thumping his chest. "To the *tavérna*. To go with them. I say *óchi*. They ask for you. For that night." He pumped his arms as if running. "I say nothing. They want to look." He gestured to the sketchpads, shrugging again. "*Léne*, 'Theofilus *eínai . . . eínai varetó.*'"

Smiling truly now, he put up his hand for her to wait and grabbed up the dictionary, thumbing through.

Her gaze traveled back to the counter, to the sketchpads. She bit her lip, a new kind of hollowness souring her stomach. At the same time she wished those boys would leave them alone, she wondered at how quickly she'd come to think of this time as theirs—hers and Theofilus's—she admitted, to think of Theofilus as hers.

A pat on her arm had her chin snapping up. Theofilus held out the dictionary, his finger on a word.

"*Varetó*," she read aloud, "is—'boring'? They called you boring?"

He nodded fast, grinning, and Kat couldn't help but grin back, especially watching him basketball-toss the dictionary onto his sleep bench. He moved behind the counter, glancing up and wiggling his eyebrows at her before closing his sketchpads. She shook her head. *What a nut!* He didn't care about Michalis and Efthimios at all.

She lifted her soda but didn't drink. Those boys were wrong. Even doing something as simple as stacking sketchpads and shoving them on a worktable, Theofilus was the *least* boring person she'd met in her life.

And right now, his face was a magnet. She had to quit staring at him. She closed her eyes, drank long and deep, wanting her insides to stop swirling and spiking but simultaneously not wanting that swirling and spiking to stop—ever.

"The running." His voice hummed in her ear. The way he spoke, syllables piling slow and steady as bricks, the *u* slanting to an *a*, made the back of her throat ache as she swallowed the bubbly lemon drink. He was trying *so* hard. "The running. Is good?"

She opened her eyes to his sunny, open expression. If *he* could forget those *vláka* boys, she could, too. "Yeah, totally *kalós*."

"Where you are running?"

"To Paralia and—" She hesitated for one beat before taking his hand and towing him up to the boat's deck.

"The mountain," she whispered, pointing up beyond the town. She thought of Artemis, Mom's stories about the gods. "Like, Olympus."

"Olympus?" he whispered back. "*Vounó eínai.*"

"'Mountain' is *vounó*?"

He nodded. "You run. To the mountain."

"Yeah," she said as they turned to each other, and the fuzzy-hot confusion of having shared her running secret with him zinged through her whole body.

"Is good," said Theofilus, his voice low. "Come."

She followed him below.

Back in the cabin, she tugged the wool strap of the *tagári* over her head.

"What this?" he said, nudging the bag.

"Just a few things." She patted the nubby wool of Artemis's face before dumping the contents out on the counter.

"You want this?" He touched a rumple of bright stretchy bathing suit.

"Swimming—yes!"

She grabbed her suit, and Theofilus walked over to a slender door, sliding it open. Scooting by, she found herself in a bathroom even more miniscule than the one at Yiayiá's.

She shimmied to get out of her sticky running gear, moving one way to keep from knocking into the toilet, then the other to avoid bashing her hip into the mini sink. She was totally naked for only a moment, but had the strange sensation that she'd slipped off the edge of her known world. Here she was. Stark naked in the middle of the night. About to go swimming in the dark with a boy she'd only known for—what was it—*three days?*

She clamped her lips tight to keep her giggles to herself, going through more contortions to tug her bathing suit on over her sweat-gummed skin.

As she peered into the small mirror to adjust the straps of her bikini top, her gaze fell to a narrow stack of shelves set into the wall. A toiletry bag sat open on the lowest shelf, the end of an orange disposable razor and the top of a can of shaving cream poking out.

She touched a finger to the shaving cream, then picked the razor out of the bag. A protector covered the blade, but tiny bits of black showed through the clear plastic. *Man!* She was obsessed. She put the razor back in the bag exactly as she'd found it.

A mixture of nerves and a desire to cool off made Kat rush up to the deck a little ahead of Theofilus. She bounded to the boat railing, ready to dive into the water.

"No," said Theofilus, pulling at her hand.

In a matter of minutes, they were down on the beach. A sliver of warm breeze came up off the water, washing against Kat's cheeks. It didn't cool her, but her shoulders twitched in a quick shiver. It was as if she and Theofilus were the only two people alive.

The second her feet hit the water, relief and pleasure swooped over her. Then she was underwater, submerged in a rush of delicious cool.

In the hush and burble, she twisted, her body slipping through the silky wet. A hand grabbed her ankle and she rolled to her back. Theofilus let go and they chased each other, laughing out loud and shushing each other. Then he ran both hands through the water, splashing her thoroughly. Barely able to see him for the spray, she splashed him back, again and again.

"*Stamáta*, Katina, stop," he said, his voice an amused, whispery plea.

She couldn't stop, wanting to play, keep playing.

He grabbed her hands in mid-splash, and they rocked side to side, their slow wrestle an easy dance.

They stopped rocking.

He kissed her.

His lips, at the same time salty and sweet, had hardly touched hers before he lifted his head, mumbling unintelligible, apologetic words. He pulled back, and the moment—*this* moment, theirs and now, *right now*—tore something inside her free.

She put her hands on his shoulders and pressed her lips to his.

CHAPTER THIRTY-TWO

Lips—bumping and hard at first, melting to soft, softer—kissing. Kissing that was not quick and good night. Kissing that was its own wrapped-up universe. Buttery and sweet. Deep and dark.

Then, the night quiet weighed heavy against her eyelids, and the *shush shush* of lapping water whispered cool against the bare skin at her waist. Her mouth—clinging, not wanting to let go—did let go, and she tipped her head back, opening her eyes.

His face loomed above, shadowed and unreadable, and she couldn't breathe.

"Katina." Only her name, whispered.

He rested his forehead against hers, and under the water, his fingers came to her hips, gentle as tiny, curious fish.

She lifted her hand, rubbing the backs of her fingers against his cheek. His warm-wet cheek, smooth, but roughness waiting, barely there, under the surface.

Again, she had the sensation of falling off the edge of her world. Lips, skin, cheeks: these things were known to her, but his were new and strange. Another country. Another planet. Her fingers roamed higher, tangling in the slick of his hair, running against his earlobe. He trembled and, whispering words she couldn't make out, lifted his forehead from hers. They kissed again, and his mouth, luscious and velvet, was no longer tentative.

After a moment, he whispered, "*Éla*," pulling her hands so that she would follow him out of the water.

The next thing she knew they were back in the dark cabin. Theofilus let her go, and Kat hugged her elbows, a bit lost. Then the *snap* of the lantern lighting.

"Cold?" He grinned, returning to chafe his hands up and down her arms.

She nodded, shivering a little from the cool night air, and a lot from what had happened in the water, from how strange and not strange it was to be with him this late into the night.

Theofilus's face went serious. He slid his hands from her arms up to her cheeks and, eyes open, leaned toward her. She kept her eyes open, too, wanting to see him in the light.

He kissed her forehead, the tip of her nose, each cheek. His mouth moved to hers, not quite touching.

"Is time. For home?" he said.

Kat nodded but didn't move, aware only that they stood close enough for their breath to mingle. He whispered three more words—three words she hadn't known she needed to hear—and rubbed his lips against hers, his hands drawing her fully against him. She hugged him back, wrapping her arms tight around his neck, her hands and elbows overlapping.

Ávrio. Óla tous, he'd said.

Yes. She closed her eyes, losing herself again. *Tomorrow. All of them.*

CHAPTER THIRTY-THREE

"Did your lips get sunburned yesterday, sweets?"

Kat jerked her fingers away from her mouth, her brain snapping back to where she was, what she was doing: sitting across from Mom at the patio table, eating a late breakfast.

"No," she mumbled, and the feeling she'd woken up with—as if the outside of her body was in one place and the inside in another—washed over her again, making everything about being with Mom weird and unreal.

"Are you sure?" Mom leaned forward, a line appearing between her eyebrows. "I think you spent too much time in the sun yesterday. That's probably why you slept this late."

She angled her coffee cup toward Kat. "I know you don't want to, but I think you should lie down during the *siesta* today. Try to sleep. Heat and jet lag can totally wipe you out."

"Yeah. Great idea."

Kat ran her tongue over her lower lip, and the night before—Theofilus's mouth moving on hers—zinged through her, making her go hot, completely raw and vulnerable. She grabbed her glass of juice and took a long swallow, sure her secrets gushed from her pores.

"You're a different person today," Mom went on. "Calm. Relaxed. It's as if you grew up overnight."

Kat coughed, almost choking on her juice.

Yes, well . . .

"I know you didn't want to come to Paralia at first, but you're really stepping up. Really helping out and going with the flow."

That's me. The old stepper-upper.

"I knew this trip was a good idea," Mom nodded, satisfied, "and I knew you wouldn't let me down."

Kat's mouth opened and closed, but she said nothing. Could say nothing. Here she was pretty much lying with every breath she took, and there was Mom, gaga about what a great daughter she had.

K at went through the motions of the morning, trying to be her normal self. Mostly she kept quiet, smiling when someone smiled at her, answering questions when someone asked her something. Lots of "stepping up" and "going with the flow." The one honestly good piece of news was that Manolis had gone back to Athens for a few days. At least she wouldn't have to deal with him and his bizarro ideas of how to treat girls.

Later in the morning they went to the beach, and when Yeorgia, Nikos, and James rushed to the water, Mom asked Kat to help set up their spot, still smiling in that relieved, too-happy way. And it was easy for her to let Mom be relieved and too happy, as if layers of thick foam wrapped everything that had happened since Kat learned of their Paralia trip, keeping it all stashed away from what—or really *who*—was at the front of her mind.

After accepting Mom's offer to rub sunscreen on her back, Kat stood and gazed out at the Aegean. Her eyes blurred with thoughts of Theofilus out on his boat, maybe casting a net or dragging one in, full of the tiny silvery fish Yiayiá loved frying.

Then the image shifted and she saw herself helping. Together they pulled and pulled at the net, and there, up in the boat's cockpit, James and Nikos stood with Kýrios Zafirakis. He showed the two boys how to steer the boat, and he smiled at them, and then smiling still, he turned to her and—

"Such a big sigh."

Kat tensed. *What was she thinking?* Spinning fantasies with Mom literally breathing down her neck.

"Don't worry, I'm almost done," Mom continued. "I know it's hard, though, your skin being this fair. It's like your father's. You *have* to use the serious sunscreen." She patted Kat's shoulder. "There, all done."

Kat held up her arms, glaring at the pinkish, lightly freckled skin under the sheerest glaze of white sunscreen. "How can I have any Greek in me at all when my skin can't take the sun here for even a second?"

Mom chuckled quietly, ducking under the umbrella.

"I mean it," Kat said, joining her. "How can I be half Greek when I don't feel *any* Greek?"

Mom regarded her a moment before speaking. "I'm not sure how to answer that, sweets."

She put her hand next to where Kat's lay on the towel. Together they studied the two hands, Mom's brown and smooth, and hers not. This time Mom let out the sigh. When she spoke, the words came slow, puzzle pieces carefully placed.

"Being Greek—or perhaps any nationality or ethnicity— isn't all about how a person looks, or even what their experience is. What I mean is, I was born here. Lived here for the first twenty-one years of my life. And then I met your father, moved to the States, and became an American citizen."

She put her hand on Kat's. "Even though I did that and then spent the next sixteen years living in Connecticut, it doesn't change the fact that inside, blood and bone, I'm Greek. It's just that now I'm American, too. And you, yes, you're American through and through." Mom took her hand away, and Kat followed its movement to her own chest, where it came to rest above her heart. "But inside here, blood and bone, whether you feel it or not, there *is* Greek."

Kat's throat tightened. She twisted to face the water. James and the cousins frolicked like three sleek brown seals. She stared down at her legs and saw Kýrios Zafirakis's disapproving glare.

"I want to belong here," she whispered, glancing back at Mom, who also watched the three in the water. "Only I-I don't know how."

Mom didn't turn her head, but her stillness told Kat she'd heard.

"It's funny you say that," Mom said after a moment. "That's exactly how I used to feel."

"That's nuts. You grew up here."

"That doesn't always seem to matter." She turned to Kat, her expression gentle, open. "I wanted a different life. That's why I went to college in England, and that's probably part of why I fell hard for your father. Except I was in such a hurry, I didn't take the time to figure out what *I* truly wanted, or where the best place for me was. I guess that's what I'm trying to do now. Give myself a restart."

Mom's words washed through Kat, something about them familiar.

"*Éla, vre* Nikos.*" James's voice rang in her ears, a cheerful little bell, and she couldn't take her eyes from him.

"James doesn't seem to have any problem 'belonging' here." Mom made a contented sound. "Yes. That's been one of the greatest things about this trip. Do you know what he told me? That he wants to come here every summer and when he's older, he and Nikos are starting a fishing business."

That James. Kat couldn't help cracking a smile.

"How come it's easy for him? You know, the Greek."

"Got me. Maybe it's because when he was a baby, I used to speak Greek to him, sing him Greek songs."

Kat's heart squeezed tight. "Didn't you do that with me?"

"I don't think I did. When you were born, I was head over heels in love with your father, with America. I think I was trying to speak only English. By the time I was pregnant with James, I guess I realized things with Dad weren't right." She paused, then let out a short laugh. "Maybe my speaking Greek with James was the start of my little rebellion."

"That kind of stinks for me," Kat said without any heat.

"It doesn't have to. You can learn Greek, too. You already are—and you're doing well. Yiayiá was telling me how proud she is of you."

Yiayiá's face delivering one of her trademark raspberries flashed behind Kat's eyes, making her grin. "Yiayiá's the best. Was she . . . was she sad when you, you know, left?"

"She was," said Mom. "She understood, though." Her voice went low and far away. "My *father*, on the other hand . . ."

"Is that what you meant before? When you said he was 'set in his ways'?"

"Yes. That would be one way to put it." This time Mom's laugh was more of a groan. "And what happened with me and my father is a big part of what I'm saying. I thought by leaving Greece, I was making my own choices, but the truth is, by rushing off the way I did, it was more like I let him make my choice for me."

She looked at Kat, her gaze steady, her smile gone. "It's your choice. I think that's what I'm trying to tell you here. Finding your Greekness, 'belonging'—anywhere, really—is about knowing yourself and choosing. It's taken me too many years to figure that out. I hope it doesn't take you as long."

Mom tugged her beach bag closer, rummaging in it, and Kat settled back on her towel, closing her eyes, something inside her trembling, trying to come clear.

People—Mom, Yiayiá, James, Dad—circled in her head, blurring until one person emerged. Herself. Herself running, the moon tinting her skin a silvery blue. She ran, and then there was Theofilus. They stood together on the beach, holding hands.

Sharp pangs nipped about the sneaking around, but none of them changed her mind about what she would be doing that night.

Her choice. That's what Mom said. Her choice to figure out how and where and why she belonged to anything. Or anybody.

CHAPTER THIRTY-FOUR

Over the next few days, Kat traveled between her two worlds. No one suspected a thing. Mom made a few comments about the size of her morning yawns, but that was about it. Volunteering for the laundry chore was pure genius. While Yiayiá hummed away over the washtub, Kat took care of hanging the wet items and folding the dry (which dried in about a second under the baking sun). It was no problem to stash her constant flow of sweaty running gear in the mountainous piles of sheets, towels, and clothes either. What was harder was keeping Theofilus to herself. His name bubbled to her lips about a gazillion times a day, begging to be said aloud, but there was no choice there. The more she thought of him, the tighter she pressed her mouth shut.

Every night, the moment Kat climbed over the fence, her body took over, and in the thrum of her steady, fast pace, any worry or confusion about her actions drained away. No choice *was* a choice, and hers was all about stealing away into the dark to run and then be with Theofilus.

Mostly he was awake when she arrived, often stretched out on his sleep bench reading or sketching. She'd come into the cabin, and he'd glance over, pushing his glasses up on his head, his grin making her insides rise, warm as Yiayiá's fresh-baked bread. First, they'd swim, so Kat could wash away the sweat from her run, then they'd hang on the beach looking at the stars. On the first night they did this, Theofilus pointed out constellations: Orion, Andromeda, Cassiopeia. The names amused Kat. Even the stars were Greek.

Back on the boat, Kat always attempted a quick stretch, and occasionally Theofilus would copy her, fake groaning and holding his lower back as if fishing was turning him into an old man. Or he'd grab his pad and pencils, studying her while he sketched. Her neck, her ear, her hand. Kat figured it was because of Kýrios Zafirakis that he never drew all of her, but the detail of those drawings? No one had ever seen her that intimately.

They also liked to sit quietly, listening to the radio, paging through Theofilus's art books. Other than school projects, Kat had never thought much about art, but the way Theofilus pored over the paintings and sculptures on each page, running his finger across a nose here, the sky there, moved her to look more closely.

Talking was slow, the Greek-English dictionary never far from their hands. They came up with a game where they'd look up a word and take turns drawing simple pictures of things about that word they liked or didn't like. The first word they picked was *family*. Theofilus drew himself painting, and then two little stick sisters standing behind with loud talk lines coming out of their mouths. Kat drew two houses on opposite ends of the page, one with Mom, James, and her inside, the other with Dad, Emma, and Shannon.

Because he had to be up super early, Kat kept her visits to about an hour, and that hour with him was like being inside a kaleidoscope, colors and shapes always moving, shifting, everything about their time together a new, ever-changing language. A language that needed fewer and fewer words.

No matter how their time went or what they did, a moment came when sitting or standing close, an inexplicable something would change. Then the kissing would start.

The kissing. At the beginning of the summer she hadn't even been able to imagine sitting in a room alone talking with, much less being touched by any boy—even a boy she thought she wanted like Mike Doherty.

Now when she looked at the picture of the New Canaan cross-country team, Mike was no more than that: a flat, thin piece of paper she couldn't believe had ever made her feel anything. How could she have known, though? What it would be like to actually be with someone? No, not just *someone*, with Theofilus.

Tonight, when she stepped into the boat's cabin, Theofilus stood with his back to the doorway. Beyond him rose the angular shape of an easel. He turned as she dropped her *tagári* on the counter.

"*Yassou*," he said, waving the paintbrush in his hand.

"*Yassou*." Almost before the word was out of her mouth, he twisted back to the easel, his smile fading in a way that told her she'd caught him in the middle of something.

She moved to his side and, without taking his eyes from the canvas, he rested his hand on the back of her neck. At once, she went bright and fizzy. She swallowed. Could he tell what happened when he touched her? That inside she vibrated like a happy puppy?

His stance pulled her thoughts away from herself. He stared at his work, quiet and concentrating, his forehead creasing as if he wasn't sure about what he saw or was maybe frustrated. She turned to the easel.

The painting was an intricate watercolor of the docks and Paralia's bustling fishing scene.

"Wow," she said. "It's great." *Great?* She frowned, wishing she could tell him, *really* tell him, what she thought.

"No," he said, gesturing with the end of his brush to different parts of the picture: the water, the dock, the faces of the fishermen. "This . . ." He spoke more, dropping his hand from her neck and moving over to the table to rummage around.

She stepped nearer to the easel. There was an odd feel to the painting. The images he pointed out did seem strange, almost otherworldly.

Theofilus came back, his leafing through the Greek-English dictionary interrupting her thoughts.

"The color. Is wrong," he began, then thumbed to another page. "Is no—true."

True. As if he'd hung the word in front, now Kat had to look at the painting through it. The colors weren't true, but to what? Then she understood. He painted the scene from memory, maybe from a bunch of memories, and that was totally different than if he could set up his art supplies in the daytime. But he had no choice. The only time he had to do his artwork was after fishing. At night. The same as her, with her running.

And maybe her running wasn't going completely as she'd planned and his painting wasn't as true as he wanted, but—

"You're doing the best you can." As she spoke, he gazed at her steadily. "I am, too. With my running." She pointed to herself, made the running motion, then reached for the dictionary. "*Prospatheí.* Understand? We're 'trying.'"

"Yes," he said with a short laugh. He tapped the side of her forehead, saying, "You *exýpni*." His fingers slid down to stroke her cheek. "*Kai oraía.*"

Smart *and* beautiful?

Full to bursting, she took the paintbrush from his hand. "Come on," she said, "let's go swimming."

A fter swimming, Kat's sense of bursting continued, pushing at her, making her restless. She didn't want to be down in the cabin, and convinced Theofilus to drag cushions up onto the deck. In the shadow of the pilothouse, she sank back, the moon, full now, hanging enormous, the rest of the sky spreading thick and velvet, a midnight blanket. Theofilus lay next to her, his warmth reaching out.

She rolled to her side as Theofilus turned his head, and just like that their mouths pressed together. She tugged at him until his body rested on hers, and the moment her lips opened under his, every part of her fell, spinning and flying in a whirling pool of his mouth tasting saltwatery and warm, his skin smelling of lemons and thyme and the sea.

His hand slid from her shoulder down, and the featherlight splay of his fingers, half on the bottom of her T-shirt, half on the bare skin of her waist, made her kiss him more furiously. His palm flexed, pressing now, traveling up under her shirt, and she clutched at his shoulders, on the brink, ready to dive, ready to—

Gunshot loud, a smacking on the dock had their mouths tearing apart.

What? Blurry, confused, Kat clung to Theofilus, about to ask that question, but he put a finger to her lips. Noises bombarded them then: rushing murmurs, hurrying feet, boards creaking and whining. Soundlessly, Theofilus rolled from her, and they both froze on their separate cushions as the whispery talk, the whispery laughter came closer.

Michalis and Efthimios.

Kat didn't need to see their faces or even to hear them clearly to know it was them.

NoNoNo! Her hand snaked up, gripping her braid, but she didn't turn her head to Theofilus. Couldn't. There was not a speck of sound from his cushion, as if they both knew that Michalis and Efthimios catching them like this would mean more than dealing with the two *vlákes*.

Feet scraping on wood, more whispering, louder now. Close. Too close. A crazy, jumbled kind of game that mixed itself up in Kat's brain. *Hide and seek, hide and seek. Come out, come out, wherever you are.* A desperate need to laugh, to scream, boiled in her throat, and she swallowed hard to hold it in, almost choking, her saliva sour on her tongue. *Peekaboo, I see you. Can't catch me. Run, run. Run and hide—*

She squeezed her eyes shut. She didn't want to play a game. Didn't want this night to be about games. *Leave, please leave.* The words chanted in her head, like counting. All she and Theofilus had to do was be quiet. *Yes!* Quiet in the dark. Everything on the boat was dark, but—but what about the lantern in the cabin? Had she and Theofilus turned it off before they came up on the deck? *Yes, of course they did.* The second those boys saw that all the lights were off, they'd leave, right?

Barely moving, Kat shifted. Theofilus stared back at her, his wide eyes telling her that he, too, was equally tense. He slid his hand to hers, and she wrapped her fingers around his. Those boys couldn't catch them. They absolutely couldn't. She and Theofilus had been careful. Always so careful. Keeping the light low when they were in the cabin, turning it off when they swam. And tonight, taking their cushions to the front of the pilothouse where they could tuck themselves away, stay hidden.

Mumbles and laughter and shuffling feet came ever closer. The *clink, clink* of a bottle. Part of Kat wanted to jump out and yell at those boys; the other part of her hated that she and Theofilus needed to hide. Hated that her insides ached with the begging wish that those boys would simply go away. *Please go away!*

The air went quiet, a held breath. Michalis and Efthimios had to be at the boat.

Thin as the glassy film of a bubble, all that stood between the boys on the dock and the two of them in the boat was one step. Kat muffled a ragged breath. But taking that step, crossing through that dark bubble skin, would be like breaking into a house. They wouldn't do that, would they? Would they?

Whispery talking, back and forth, high, then low. Arguing. Yes. It was late, way late. *Go home! Go to bed!* Wait, "bed." One of them said "*kreváti*," the Greek word for "bed." One of them cared that Theofilus was a fisherman and didn't want to wake him up. Then a hissing, scoffing *pfft* of breath answered by a whispered "*Éla*," and footsteps, footsteps. Retreating now.

Kat strained to hear every move, every sound. Quiet descended, a thick fog. They were gone.

For a long moment, Theofilus stared into Kat's eyes, then he blew out a long breath, his hand coming to her cheek. "Home now?" he whispered.

Fingers trembling, she covered his hand. *So sweet.* That he would want her home and safe. And he was right. She *should* go home. That was the smart thing to do.

"I take you," he said, stroking her skin. "*Éla.*"

"No, wait," she said, "wait." Sensations swelled in her, up

through the fizz of anger at those boys ruining their night, up through the wash of relief at not being caught, and she burned. Burned with what she and Theofilus had been doing before they'd been interrupted, burned with what she *still* wanted even now.

"I don't want to go home yet," she whispered. "I . . ." She took his hand from her cheek and placed his open palm against her chest.

CHAPTER THIRTY-FIVE

Steeped in dream shadows, Kat woke to the now familiar breakfast noises of silverware *chunk chunking* against dishes and voices murmuring in Greek. She yawned and rolled to her back, stretching her arms over her head. Under the sheet, she straightened her legs, pointing her toes. A cramp clenched her calf, and she kicked the sheet aside, flexing her foot and rubbing the sore spot. All the hill climbing was beating on her calves. She needed to stretch more, *should* stretch right after running. Except last night . . .

Last night she'd been busy right after running—she mentally thumbed her nose at the blip of Michalis and Efthimios's little appearance—*real* busy.

Grabbing her pillows, Kat plumped them against the wall, snuggling back. Well, not *that* busy. She and Theofilus were not ready for *that*, but—*wow*. She touched her breasts, and even through her sleep shirt the skin tingled as if naked, remembering. She remembered, too. Her hand putting his on her chest—*did she really do that?*—and the kissing, so much kissing, making her breathless, making her ache. Then his palm sliding up under her shirt, over her ribs; fingertips undoing the tie at the back of her bikini and moving to the underside of her breast. She thought she would die.

Could someone die from feeling that good?

Now she let her own fingers trace the path his had taken, and she shivered, a giddy little quake. How different that skin felt from any other skin, the untouched-ness making it beyond sensitive.

Beads clacking at her doorway had her snatching her hands away.

"Katina *mou*." Yiayiá peeked in. "Good morning."

Kat stretched her arms and legs in every direction as if only now opening her eyes. "Good morning, Yiayiá."

"You have things?" Yiayiá pointed to the laundry basket under her arm. "For washing?"

"Um." Kat glanced over the edge of her mattress, startling at the sight of the *tagári*—spilling its contents—and her running shoes and gear tumbled in a careless clump. *What was wrong with her?* It was as if she wanted to get caught.

"Sure. Yeah," she said. "I'll bring it." Heart drumming, she rose, casually dragging at her sheet so it would drape over most of the pile on the floor. "And I'll be right there. To help."

"Is okay," Yiayiá said, brows drawing together over those owlish eyes. "No hurry."

"Perfect." Kat threw Yiayiá a hopefully relaxed-looking smile, not moving until she was alone and the door-curtain hung motionless. Then she blew out a sharp breath and, flipping the sheet back on the bed, plucked her socks from her running shoes and balled them, along with her running shorts, tank, and bra, into a clammy wad. Next, she yanked up the *tagári*, goggling at Artemis as she dumped the bag on the bed. Out fell her brush and the small towel. Where was her—? There. From under the bed poked a bright lump of bikini. She snatched it up, saw it was only the bottom, and lowered to all fours. She peeked under the bed, and her insides swooped as if a trapdoor swung open under her. Her bikini top was nowhere in sight.

Dropping her sweaty pile, Kat crawled around the bed, scrambling, searching. Nothing. She shook the empty *tagári*, pawed through her running gear, stripped the sheet off the bed. And froze, all at once remembering. Her own hand undoing the tie at her neck and pulling the top away. Her own hand, pale and blue in the moonlight, tossing it off to the side. To some dark corner of the deck. Where it still had to be.

The sheet slipped from Kat's fingers, her breathing coming short and labored, like she was running up the mountain road. She'd left her bikini top on the boat. On the boat that now had to be way out at sea. And there was nothing she could do, except hope that Theofilus had found the top while doing his morning chores.

Blindly, she sat on the edge of the mattress, imagining him emerging on to the boat's deck, the light sunrise soft. Blushed thinking of him discovering her top, of him remembering them tangled together on the cushions.

But that's what *must've* happened. After all, that was why he slept on the boat, right? To get it all ready for fishing? She tried to laugh, but the sound that barked out was more of a strangled choke. Of *course*, he found her top. Because if *he* hadn't found it—*oh, God!*

She grabbed for her water bottle, fumbling with the cap. When she finally got it open, she sucked water down her throat almost faster than she could swallow.

No matter what Mom said about choices, there was no choice about tonight. The only place she would be running was right to the boat. Right to Theofilus to make sure their secret was safe.

Finally, finally it was late enough for her to be out the window and over the fence.

Specks of light shone from every direction, as it was only a little after 11:00 p.m.—much earlier than she usually ran. Kat missed her familiar dark. Twice she had to duck down on the beach when the high beams of a passing car swung her way. At least there weren't any motorbikes.

Running the mile to Paralia seemed to take forever. At last, she made it, the music and laughter spilling from the busy *tavérna* causing her heart to pound that much more unevenly.

Scurrying to the docks, she raced onto the boat, breathing in the now-familiar lemony-thyme scent. The tightness in her chest loosened. *Okay.* Everything seemed the way it always was, looking exactly as it was all supposed to look.

She hurried to the cabin, her feet moving so fast down the steps that she almost tripped herself.

"Theofilus!"

He jerked, dropping his book. "Katina?" One look at her had him jumping to his feet.

She threw herself against him, wrapping her arms around his neck, beyond glad that the cabin was the same and quiet and safe and—

The door above creaked and heavy steps rushed down, a shout exploding.

"Theofilus!"

Kýrios Zafirakis.

For a second, for an eternity, nothing and no one moved.

Then Kat fell away from Theofilus's chest, and Kýrios Zafirakis stalked over, yelling in Greek that pounded loud as Yiayiá's knife slamming against the cutting board, shaking his fist in Theofilus's face. His fist that was full of the bikini top.

Shaking it and shaking it, like that small bit of fabric was the dirtiest piece of garbage.

Kat shrank back, watching Theofilus's expression go from startled beige confusion, to deep angry red, to scary frozen pale. At the same time, she didn't know what to do and she knew there was nothing she *could* do.

Now Theofilus tried to talk to him, his voice hushed in a way that was so much worse than Kýrios Zafirakis's harsh tone. Kat stared at the floor in agony. Every time Theofilus said, "Katina," and every time Kýrios Zafirakis answered with, "Kyría Sofia" or "Kyría Maria" or "American," it was as if nails drove into her heart.

Her bikini top hit the counter with a slap, and Kat looked up, trying to think of anything she could say. Kýrios Zafirakis was already across the cabin, though, standing rigid in front of the sleep bench, his back to them both, his fists clenched rock hard on his hips.

She reached to touch Theofilus's arm, but he drew away without meeting her eyes, striding to the table to rummage furiously through his art supplies.

What was happening? Kat wanted to ask that question as much as she didn't want to know the answer. She picked up her bikini top with her fingertips, as though the fabric would bite, and glanced to the door. Her feet longed to run away, but she couldn't. Couldn't leave Theofilus to deal with his grandfather alone.

Her eyes darted from Kýrios Zafirakis's stiff, unmoving back to Theofilus, now stuffing a small sketchpad and pencil in his back pocket. A beat later, he hurried to her side, saying, "Come."

Kýrios Zafirakis shot around. "*Óchi*, Theofilus!" He barked a bunch of commands.

Theofilus took her elbow. "Come," he repeated.

Kýrios Zafirakis marched over and grabbed Theofilus's other arm, stabbing a finger toward her, his dismissive tone a clear message that he didn't want Theofilus to go anywhere with her. Theofilus squared his shoulders and spoke in the kind of quiet, firm voice that made Kat think of brave knights in shining armor.

With a disgusted *hiss* of breath, Kýrios Zafirakis threw away Theofilus's arm, waving them both off as if they were a cloud of foul smoke.

Out on the road, Kat practically had to run to keep up with Theofilus.

"Theofilus." She gripped his arm. "Wait—please."

He stopped short, and she knocked into his side, almost tumbling to the ground. He steadied her but let go fast, shoving his hands in his pockets and turning away to gaze out at the sea. Sadness rose off him thick as steam, overwhelming her. It wasn't only that they'd been caught; Theofilus had let down his *pappoús*.

Kat imagined the shock on Mom's and Yiayiá's faces when they found out what she'd been up to. She tried to swallow but couldn't, a harsh, over-lit image of the cabin just now—Kýrios Zafirakis storming in—flaring in her head. She winced, seeing everything through his eyes, the eyes of Mom and Yiayiá. Nasty, sleazy, lying girl. Exactly like the girls in her stupid books and like the "American girls" Michalis and Efthimios claimed to know all about.

"I'm sorry." The words fell out of her mouth, a quiet sob. "I'm so sorry, Theofilus."

"No," he said, shaking his head. He came to her and put his hands on her shoulders. "I-I don't have words."

He blew out a breath that became a frustrated little laugh and hugged her close. Her arms slid around his waist. She pressed her forehead tight to his, stealing one moment to rest in the relief that he didn't hate her.

Too soon they reached Yiayiá's gate, but Kat didn't want to say good night—the weight of how much she didn't want to like heavy, dragging sandbags.

She opened her mouth, but he put his finger to her lips, pulling out the sketchbook and pencil, writing furiously. When he finished, he ripped out the paper, tucking it in her hand.

"What?" she began, but he put his finger over her lips again.

Then he kissed her, slow and gentle. As his head lifted, her insides rushed, startled birds flushed from their nest. Her lips followed the retreat of his, wanting to cling.

"*Antío*, Katina."

Not ávrio, *not tomorrow.*

She stood there clutching the paper, hurt flooding her, drowning her.

"Goodbye," she whispered, but he'd already disappeared down the lane.

CHAPTER THIRTY-SIX

Through the night Kat was sure Kýrios Zafirakis would show up, that Mom and Yiayiá would burst into her room demanding an explanation. Hour after hour nothing happened, and eventually Kat slumped into a half-asleep haze that, when morning finally broke, left her dull and exhausted.

Now she perched on a marble step, helping Yiayiá with the after-breakfast chore of trimming dead leaves and stems from her endless pots of geraniums. Every time Kat shifted, though, she could hear the crinkle of paper in her pocket. Theofilus's note.

She'd opened the note last night, but of course it was in Greek, and of course she couldn't read it. Even so, she'd examined the dips and swirls of the familiarly unfamiliar script, tracing Theofilus's words with her finger and thinking of finding letters from Yiayiá on the kitchen counter back home, of Mom talking to James in Greek, singing to him. And she wished. Wished that whatever bit of Greek was in her *could* understand these words, this language, just this once.

She still wished that now. With a sigh, Kat made a pile of yellow and brown leaves, then used the small clippers Yiayiá gave her to snip off the dead flowers. Except wishing wasn't going to help her find out what the note said. There was only one person she could ask for help—Yeorgia.

She'd been thinking of Yeorgia's help all morning, had almost rushed over to the other cottage a dozen times. Another thought had stopped her, though. Could she ask Yeorgia to keep such a secret?

Yiayiá joined her on the step. "*Kalós*," she said, "you do good work."

Kat smiled a little and kept snipping.

"You have flowers like this," Yiayiá went on, "in Connecticut?"

"No," Kat said. "I mean, *naí*, we *did* have flowers. Except not these." She pointed to the geraniums. "Mom hasn't done any planting. Since the new house." She glanced up at Yiayiá. "The new *spíti*. Understand?"

"Aaaah, *naí*." Yiayiá nodded. "Don't worry. Your *mamá*. She have them again. She like flowers."

"I guess."

"These grow here." Yiayiá waved her own clippers at the geraniums. "Grow there. *Polý dynató*. You remember *dynató*?"

Used to Yiayiá's mix of Greek and English that said one thing but seemed to say another, Kat went along. "Sure," she said, flexing her bicep, patting it. "Super strong. Like me, right, Yiayiá?"

Yiayiá tipped her head back and laughed. Then she cupped Kat's cheek, her thumb rubbing the place below Kat's eye. "You *look* tired, but you strong," she said, "strong helper."

Watching Yiayiá continue down the steps, Kat resisted the urge to touch her pocket, feel the stiff fold of the note within. Instead, she turned back to the pot before her, studying the bright red blooms. "Strong," Yiayiá had called them, and she was right. Kat had seen pots of geraniums in front of plenty of New Canaan houses. She frowned. Did it matter to the flowers? Where they grew? She shook her head at herself. *Don't be dumb.*

Flowers couldn't think. They were just flowers. Still, she stroked a finger over a soft, moist petal and flicked a quick look at Yiayiá, now bending over more pots in the yard. Maybe flowers *were* just flowers, but look how amazing they could be: probably able to grow almost anywhere on the planet. Anywhere someone took the time to water them, to care for them.

The gate opened and Theía Tassia came in, followed by Yeorgia. Kat's chest tightened at Yeorgia's cheery wave. This time Kat didn't resist the urge, putting her hand in her pocket and clutching the paper.

There was no other option. She had to ask Yeorgia for help. Heat crept up her neck as she imagined Yeorgia reading Theofilus's words, knowing her secrets.

Theía Tassia stopped to chat with Yiayiá, and Yeorgia paused where James and Nikos lay in the yard playing cards.

Kat bit her lip as she walked over. Yeorgia looked very young standing there watching the boys, her arms clasped behind her back. No matter what Theofilus had written, Yeorgia would freak at what Kat had been up to.

"Yeorgia?"

Yeorgia turned, bright and expectant.

Kat swallowed and spoke in a low voice. "I need to talk to you for a minute."

The two of them headed to Kat's room, and when Kat stopped to hold her beaded curtain aside, Mom came around the side of the cottage. They caught eyes and Mom's smile was instant and warm, expressing, *See how easy it is to get along with your Greek cousins? I'm proud of you.*

Kat shot Mom a brief smile in return, her lips stiff, shellacked to her face. *If she only knew.* Except Kat didn't want her to know. Didn't want her ever to know.

In her room, Kat drew Theofilus's note from her pocket and held it out.

Yeorgia cocked her head as she took the paper, unfolding it as if it were a priceless treasure map. She couldn't have read more than a couple of words before her chin snapped up.

"Katina? What is this?" she said, breathy with shock.

"Please, Yeorgia. I need to know what it says."

After blinking at her for another second, Yeorgia bent her head again.

For the next few moments, the only sound in the room was the light rustling of paper. Kat couldn't look at Yeorgia as she read, instead fixing her gaze on the doorway. *Please don't let anyone come in.*

When Yeorgia blew out a long breath, Kat knew she was finished, but, fear twisting, she still couldn't look at her right away. Now Kat would know what Theofilus wanted her to know. Possibly the *last* something he wanted her to know.

"Well?"

"He say . . ." Yeorgia dropped her eyes back to the page. Kat could see that both of her hands shook. "Theofilus apologize about his *pappoús*. That he is yelling so much. He say that you will not come anymore. At night. To the boat. And if you stop, his *pappoús* will not tell Kyría Maria and Kyría Sofia. He say his *pappoús* will make him go to Athens *now* if you don't keep away."

A faint buzzing began in Kat's head, growing louder as what Yeorgia said sank in. *Kýrios Zafirakis wouldn't tell, but only if she—if he and she—*

"He say he can't go to Athens now. He need this job. For money." Yeorgia paused, the noise of her swallow crackling in Kat's ears. "And he say he is sorry. He wish you to run up the mountain. He leave his street, the number. For a letter."

She thrust Theofilus's note into Kat's hand, staring at her, tight-lipped and goggle-eyed. Kat felt as if she'd turned her cousin into a stone-cold statue, like in that Greek myth James had showed her about an ugly-as-*skatá*, snake-headed creature called Medusa that froze anyone who saw her with one look.

"Katina, what is this?" Yeorgia huffed out a frustrated little *pfft* of air. "You and Theofilus." She continued in Greek peppered with enough references to the entire family *and* Kýrios Zafirakis that Kat needed no translation. *What was she thinking? Everyone would freak out if they knew she'd been sneaking around at night with Theofilus. Was she in love? Or simply crazy, nuts, loco?*

"Yeorgia," Kat tried to interrupt, but Yeorgia didn't stop until Kat put her hand over the girl's mouth. "I know," she said, "I know. I'm crazy."

Yeorgia pushed Kat's hand from her mouth. "Yes. You and Theofilus. Both crazy. What you will do?"

Kat tugged on her braid, everything Theofilus wrote churning in her brain. How he needed the money from the fishing job for Italy. How Kýrios Zafirakis wouldn't say anything to Mom or Yiayiá if they stayed away from each other.

"I-I don't know," she said finally. "There's nothing *to* do. Nothing."

Yeorgia clicked her tongue, and then Kat felt her hand on her shoulder. "Is better," she said, giving Kat a gentle rub. "Sneaking around with boys. Is no good."

Except sneaking around with Theofilus *had* been good. Had been the best! Except—Kat yanked her braid hard, harder, making her scalp sting—except for being too lame to remember her *vlákas* bikini top. Except for Kýrios catching them. Except for Theofilus's downcast face.

Kat refolded the note and numbly placed it back in her

pocket. Theofilus. He'd wished her luck running up the mountain, because he understood how important it was to her. That was something. She'd make it to the top all right. Not even mean, nasty Kýrios Zafirakis could take that away. Her running. That was still safe, still hers.

CHAPTER THIRTY-SEVEN

D ear Theofilus,
I know you won't get this until you get home, but I

Kat crossed out what she'd written and tapped her pen against her lip. She couldn't get Theofilus out of her mind. Everything that had happened—from that first day when she'd seen him in the water until last night when he'd said *antío*—going around and around in her head, a mad-crazy gerbil on a wheel.

Man! What had Kýrios Zafirakis done to him when he'd gotten back to the boat?

If only she could talk to Theofilus. Ask him if he was okay. Apologize again.

Since that morning, she'd pored over his note a dozen times, the only part she recognized at the bottom. Three short lines mixed with numbers. His address.

Now it was past dinner, getting later by the second, and she still didn't know what to say. But she had to say something. *Had to.*

She held her pen, hovering, then wrote:

Hi Theofilus,
This is really hard. I wish I could talk to you

She crossed this out, too, pressing her pen down until she'd slashed every word shiny with ink. He'd given her his address; that meant he must want her to write, but what good would writing him do now? He wouldn't get her letter until the end of the summer, and he wouldn't be able to read her words. He'd have to find a translator—like she found Yeorgia—and that made everything totally lame and weird.

Besides—she tore the page of cross-outs into confetti, shoving the illegible bits into the stationery box—she wanted to *be* with him, not write to him. Her hand flopped to where the *tagári* sat on the bed next to her thigh, her fingers finding the wool stitches forming the coil of Artemis's hair. Through the fabric, she traced the spiral binding of the *Runner's Journal. Maybe . . .* she pulled the bag open, tugged the journal out. Maybe she couldn't talk to Theofilus in person, but what if she could?

She opened the journal, turning to a fresh page.

Hi,

I am really sorry everything got so screwed up, and I hope your grandfather isn't too mad at you. I just wish I could talk to you without this big language problem. Maybe someday I'll know how to speak Greek and you'll know how to speak English, then look out, world!

Anyway, I hope you earn tons of money this summer, and get to go to Italy. That's super important. You are such a good artist! Don't let anyone talk you out of it. I wish your grandfather knew that. Does he have any idea how negative he is? Ha! Maybe that's why his other son moved so far away. (I guess I'm glad you can't read that, but I'm MAD!!)

Oh well, I'm glad I met you, and I will keep running and I will get to the top of the mountain. I will. I only wish—

A knock outside her door had her slapping the journal shut.

"Kat?" Mom came in as Kat capped her pen. "There you are! We're about to—" She frowned, taking in the room. "It's kind of dark in here, sweets. What are you doing?"

"Nothing," Kat said, tucking the journal back into the *tagári*. "I guess I'm a little tired."

"You've seemed tired all day." Mom sat on the edge of the bed. "This heat is taking more of a toll on you than I thought it would. You must be extra sensitive."

"Yeah, I guess you're right. Hey, why are you dressed up?"

"Boy, you really *are* tired. I told you earlier—Theía Tassia ran into a couple of friends at the market this morning, and they invited us over for an after-dinner drink. They live on the other side of the mountain, so we'll be a little late. Of course, James will be here, but Tassia wondered if it would be okay if Yeorgia and Nikos came over here instead of staying at their cottage and, since you're the oldest . . ."

Mom let her sentence trail off, and her expression took Kat's breath for a moment. "You mean," Kat said finally, "you mean, you guys trust *me* to babysit everyone?"

"Yes. Of course we do. We'd be back around midnight."

Mom's face was so lit up, so confident and sure, that at that moment Kat wanted to deserve Mom's trust.

"Okay," she said, making herself smile, "you got it."

"I knew I could count on you," said Mom, patting her knee. "The other kids are playing cards. Why don't you come out and join them?"

Temper Control was one of those twisty-turny card games played with multiple decks where all the players had to pay close attention. The kind of close attention Kat's wandering brain couldn't muster. She was losing big, had been all night.

"All *right*, Nikos!" said James, slapping Nikos's back, then smirking at Kat. "You have to pick up four, Kat."

"No way. I thought 3s meant switch directions!"

Both James and Nikos shook their heads, their glee ferocious.

"No," said Yeorgia, "a 3 mean the next person need the 4. You have a 4, Nikos pick up three cards. *Óchi* the 4, you need four cards. You have this 4?"

"No," muttered Kat.

She shot James and Nikos her double hairy eyeball and snapped up four cards. She was supposed to be getting rid of cards, but now had about a deck's worth. She looked at her watch. *Groan.* 8:30 p.m. They'd been playing cards forever.

"This game is getting old, guys. How about we—"

Yiayiá's gate creaked open, but it wasn't Mom and the others back too soon; it was Manolis, back from Athens.

"*Yassou,*" he called, bounding up the steps.

He plunked down on the bench, sliding over until he was right next to Kat.

Her instincts told her to bolt away, but with Yeorgia on her other side, she was stuck.

Well, wasn't this perfect? She glanced at Yeorgia, smiling a little when Yeorgia crossed her eyes.

"What is this game?" said Manolis, leaning over her shoulder. *This guy had no sense of personal space.*

Kat put her cards down, and he picked them up, turning to ask James and Nikos about the game.

She was about to ask Yeorgia to move so that she could get out, when a sweaty palm landed on her knee.

Shocked as if by a rogue zap of electricity, Kat could only stare, first down at the hand, then up into the too-close, too-everything-repulsive face of Manolis. She jerked her knee free.

"Katina," he said, unfazed, his lips rubbery as they stretched away from his teeth. "This game look boring. *Éla.* Come to my house. I bring you something from Athens. I want to show you."

His hand on her thigh now, squeezing.

She stood fast, her hip jamming against the table. Cards went flying. James, Nikos, and Yeorgia gaped at her.

"What is wrong?" said Manolis, on his feet, too.

"Don't give me that!" She smacked the table. "You know exactly 'what is wrong'!"

"There is a mistake."

The way he looked at her, eyes flat as a waiting snake's, made her snap.

"You are *so* full of it! There's no mistake."

"I think"—his voice went low and cajoling—"we need to talk about this. Alone. *Éla,* we go for a walk. I know you like to walk. At night." Then, there it was—that self-satisfied, lip-pursing smirk again.

Kat's hand shot up, ready to wipe that smile off his face, but his hand caught her wrist, his fingers wrapping it tight.

"What is with you?" she said, shaking his hand off. "You think you can do whatever you want because you know a big secret about me?" She rubbed her wrist, all but vibrating with anger and disbelief. "You don't know anything about me. Nothing!"

He lifted his shoulders in a clownish, exaggerated shrug. "I don't know what you are talking about."

Man, she hated that know-it-all voice!

"That's just it!" Kat threw her arms wide. "Maybe if you

actually tried to get to know me, instead of showing off for your friends and playing stupid games, we could be—" She broke off, sighing loud and long. "We *could* have been friends."

His eyebrows rose, his mouth pouting like a little boy whose favorite toy has been snatched away. The change gave her a speck of hope that she was finally getting through to him.

"Come *on*, Manolis. It's so obvious. You only want to be with me to impress your stupid friends. But that's not how it works. That's not—" The rest of her sentence froze on her tongue, her running-goddess fantasy spiraling in her brain. *Gah!*

The sound of a chair leg scraping snapped Manolis's gaze from her face. In one silent moment, his eyes flicked from James and Nikos to Yeorgia, and he seemed to shrink. Then his shoulders shuddered as if he were shaking off a chill, and he straightened.

"You are mistaken, Katina," he said, his reptile face back. He retreated toward the steps, smoothing his shirt collar, his hair. "Kyría Maria and Kyría Sofia will *not* like hearing you are speaking to me this way."

The frustration of the day caught up with her then, flooding out the gate after him at top volume. "You go right ahead, Manolis! Tell my mom and Yiayiá anything you want. I-I don't even care anymore!"

She pushed past Yeorgia and hurried to her room, wishing more than anything she had an actual door to slam.

Kat paced her tiny room, but two steps one way, two steps the other wasn't cutting it. She stopped, her whole body a silent scream, ready to explode. *Gah!* She dropped onto her bed. How could she have been that stupid? About Mike and the New

Canaan team, about Theofilus, about *everything*. She threw on her running clothes and fumbled under the bed for her running shoes. She needed to clear her head, and going for a run was the only way. Running. Right now.

A light knock came, but she didn't answer, silently tying one shoe and reaching for the other.

The knock came again, this time louder. "Katina?" Quiet, worried Yeorgia.

"Please. Leave me alone, Yeorgia."

"What is all this with Manolis?"

"I don't want to talk about him now. I-I'm tired. I'm going to—" As Kat said, "bed," Yeorgia came in, instantly taking in her running gear.

"What you are doing?"

"You don't want to know." Kat jerked her laces into a double knot and sprang to her feet.

"You go somewhere? Now? *Óchi*, Katina. You cannot do this. You and Theofilus cannot—"

"I'm *not* going to see Theofilus. But I am going running."

Eyeing Yeorgia, Kat grabbed her water bottle and took a long drink. "Look, I wasn't going to tell you I was going, because I didn't want you to have to lie for me, but it's okay—I do this every night. I won't run that far. Just a little beyond the town. I'll be back in half an hour."

"Katina." Yeorgia gazed at her as though she'd sprouted horns, and she shook her head. "*Óchi*."

"Half an hour," Kat repeated. She gulped more water. "It's 8:45 p.m. now. I'll be back by 9:15—9:30 p.m. tops. Way before everyone gets back. You be in charge for a little while. But don't tell James and Nikos, okay? Say I went to bed."

She slapped the water bottle on the bedside table and

grabbed her flashlight, but she couldn't leave with Yeorgia staring at the floor like that.

"Yeorgia, please." Kat dipped her head to get Yeorgia to look her in the eye. "This is the only time I can run, and you know Mom and Yiayiá would *never* let me go out this late. Running's important to me—and I know you understand. Remember, *pilótos?*"

Yeorgia's chin came up. "Is not the same," she said, small and quivery. "I don't lie."

Kat let out an unhappy little breath. "You're right. You don't. But you're not exactly telling your parents the truth about what *you* want either."

Silence hung a moment, then Yeorgia said, "Okay, you go." She made a shooing motion with her hands. "But you come back fast."

"You're the best," said Kat, hugging her. "Don't worry, I'll be back in half an hour. Promise."

She slid over the windowsill, gave Yeorgia a thumbs-up, and tiptoe-ran around the back of the house.

CHAPTER THIRTY-EIGHT

Voices coming from Marula's house stopped Kat at Yiayiá's back gate. Marula and Manolis, out on their patio. *Crap!* No matter how quiet she was, where they stood—too close to the railing—made it more than likely that even in the shadowy light they would see her dash across the empty lot.

She waited, suspended. If only they'd take their conversation inside, except Marula sounded pretty angry. Kat couldn't make out what was going on, but now it looked like Marula was pushing a bundle at Manolis, saying, "*Vlákas . . . kefáli . . .*"

Stupid head? Ha! If Marula only knew how right she was.

Kat flinched as, with a fierce exclamation, Manolis grabbed whatever it was Marula shoved at him and strode out of sight. A second later, his motorbike choked to life and roared down the lane.

Kat watched Marula inch her way around the patio, tidying up and extinguishing the lights one by one. When she came to the final light, Marula looked toward the lane, saying Manolis's name and more, as if the night could carry her words to him. Leaving this last light on, she shuffled inside the house.

Kat slipped through the gate and bolted across the lot. Poor Marula. Did she have any idea what a sleazebag her grandson was? Maybe *Kat* should tell her, but—man, what a conversation *that* would be.

Kat's fingers scraped and stung in her hurry to scrabble over the fence and get going. Manolis's motorbike was long out of earshot, but even so she wished she could make herself invisible for this short half hour or will it that no cars, no motorbikes, *no one* would pass her on the road.

She looked at the sky as she ran down the hill. The waning moon loomed above, not nearly as fat as a full moon, but still round and white and huge. The moon. Didn't Artemis wear a moon on her crown? Kat hunched her shoulders, her back feeling bare and empty without the *tagári*. In her mind's eye, she saw the white wool moon perched above Artemis's head. It wasn't a full-moon shape. No. It was a perfect crescent resting on its side, a smile, at the same time both encouraging and powerful. *Please, Artemis.* She ran faster. *Let me run, please.*

Then she was almost to Paralia, and no one *had* passed her. As she got closer, the lights, music, and laughter of the *tavérna* reached out, invisible threads spiraling around her. Even from a distance, she could see people hanging around the entrance, talking and smoking.

Veering off the road, she headed inland across rocky scrub. When she got near the *tavérna*, she noted the slew of motorbikes parked along the side, smelled their oily engine burn. Flashes of Helmet-Man, Michalis, Efthimios, and Manolis strobed behind her eyes, but she kept going, ducking farther into the shadows around the back of the *tavérna*, the back of the market.

When she was well past the buildings, she returned to the road and couldn't help glancing over her shoulder, searching for the lights near the docks. *Theofilus.* If only she had a way to send him a message, tell him she was out, right now, running. Maybe then he'd look up at the moon and know she was heading for the mountain. She imagined him wishing her luck.

The moment she began to go up the mountain road, breathing became hard. Too hard. *Love the running. Love the running.* Only, the air was hotter than on previous nights, as though secret pockets of dark held the sun's heat. She had to distract herself. Visualize. Not about the *vlákas* star-runner stuff; about something chilly and refreshing.

The sea. How she'd seen it that first time from Theíos Nick's car. For a second Kat's body cooled, as if imagining the color of the water—that perfect blue—had plunged her deep into it. What was it Theíos Nick had said the other day? About why the water was this particular blue? That there was a special kind of seaweed found only in the Aegean? Or that there was no seaweed?

Maybe no one knew, and maybe it didn't matter what mix of plants or fish or whatever made the water impossibly blue, but only that all the jumbling together made this sea unique in the world.

She saw herself in the water, swimming and playing with Theofilus, and ached with how much she longed to meet him later at the boat.

Then there, she went by the spiky bush, her first landmark.

Kýrios Zafirakis. The name stabbed at her with each step. Who was he to tell them they couldn't see each other? As though he controlled everything, everyone? Who gave him that power?

Like a whisper, *You did.*

Was that true? Was it?

Higher and higher she climbed, her heart knocking against

her ribs, her breath coming faster and shorter, cutting itself smaller, smaller.

There had to be a way to take that power back. A way she and Theofilus could keep seeing each other without messing up his job. Without messing up her running.

Higher and higher. There, her next landmark, the boulder now.

Choices. That's what Mom had told her. She had to know what she wanted and choose what to do. Except, what if she screwed everything up again? What if—? *Stop. Stop thinking and run.*

But she couldn't stop the place deep inside her that yearned for a bit of magic, a sign, *anything.*

Artemis. Kat watched the moon again, wishing answers would materialize in the crags and shadows. Silvery and motionless, the waning disk remained a mirror of her unknowing.

Fine. She'd figure out her own sign when she reached the top. She spotted an olive grove and, fingers shaking, saluted it as she moved by. Yes, the very instant she reached the top.

Kat glued her eyes to the road, trying to ignore the stinging pains shooting up through the soles of her feet into her calves, trying to ignore the shallow rasp of her breathing. She wanted to stop. Had to stop. *No.* She shook her head, her braid swinging on her shoulders like a horse's mane. Distraction. More distraction. But when *would* she get to the top anyway? When?

The top. She almost choked on her breath. *That* was the sign. *That* was the deal. If she made it to the top of the mountain—*tonight*—that meant she should find Theofilus and come up with a plan to keep seeing him. Even if part of that plan meant Mom and Yiayiá found out about the running, about the sneaking out, about everything. If she didn't make it, that meant they shouldn't be together.

She had to make it.

Kat pushed herself past the pain in her legs, past the struggle to breathe. *One more step. Love the running, love the running. One more, one more.*

She was hardly moving now, her feet rising and falling, tapping at the road like a kid with a tiny hammer. Everything in her wanted to collapse. Wanted to lie down in the middle of the dust and dry of the pavement and let go. She imagined herself doing exactly that, and could all but feel the relief of it. Her body kept running, though. Kept running. Up the mountain. Into the dark. Up. Dark. Up. Dark.

Man, it was dark up here.

Dark. And dizzying. Dizzying and dark.

Kat took her next step and, in one weightless swoop, almost fell forward as the steep of the road leveled. Panting, she stopped, her blurred vision wheeling, adjusting. Then she stumbled forward, and the horizon burst open before her.

Hilly terrain spread out, far and wide as her eyes could see, a thick, dark carpet, tiny lights dotting a path that led away to the distant glow of other towns, maybe other cities. Barely visible beyond that faraway glow, the triangular shapes of other mountains rose to where the edge of the gleaming sky bent to meet them.

Kat's shaking fingers found their way to her mouth, her shivery insides wanting to laugh and cry. She'd made it to the top of the mountain. She'd *made it*, and it was beautiful. So, so beautiful and amazing and . . .

Endless. A soft laugh escaped through her lips, echoing in her head, breaking her heart. Everything kept going and going. Up and down and up again. Magic.

And at the same time, not magic.

Flashlight still gripped in her fist, Kat wrapped her arms around herself, hugging her trembly body tight.

Like making choices. Like finding answers. Like being alive!

Tipping her head up to the ever-expanding night sky, she smiled at the moon.

Yes. Magic and not magic. Her life. Packed into her wobbling, shaking, stronger-than-anything body. Everything she wanted. Everything she needed. Everything she was, and could be. Clear at this moment. Moon-bright clear.

CHAPTER THIRTY-NINE

K at hurried along the docks. She needed to see Theofilus. Needed to tell him she wanted to keep seeing him. Needed to tell him so many things.

Near the boat, she slowed. The air felt different here, crackly and waiting. Instead of rushing onboard, she crouched by a porthole. The lantern inside was lit, but the cabin was empty. Then the bathroom door opened.

Kýrios Zafirakis!

She fell back on her hands, the metal of her flashlight skittering as she scooted away.

Why was Kýrios on the boat? *Did that mean—? No.* Theofilus couldn't be back in Athens already. He couldn't be!

The tiny cottage with the copper fish weathervane flashed into her head.

K at had almost reached the road leading up to the cottages when sweeping lights coming from behind forced her to dive down to the beach. She sprawled belly-down, flattening herself to avoid the headlights' glare. *Please don't let it be Theíos Nick's car.* The car tore by, continuing along the road like a roaring magic carpet. The second the car vanished from sight, she popped up, racing to Kýrios Zafirakis's lane.

Her spirits leapt when she saw light glowing from the Zafirakis cottage. She pushed through the gate, craning her head to look through the front windows.

Theofilus sat at a small table bent over his sketchpad. When she knocked on the glass, his startled frown shifted instantly to a wide grin.

"Katina?" He dashed out the door, pulling her into a hug.

"You are crazy."

"Yeah, completely." She buried her face in his neck, breathing him in.

Then he was kissing her. She let herself sink in for a moment, before drawing away.

"Theofilus. I-I want you and me." She pointed to him, before clasping her hands over her heart. "Together."

"I want this, too." He shook his head. "But Pappoús say no."

"It's not up to him." She grabbed his hand. "I want to tell my mom and Yiayiá everything. Everything about us."

"Everything? Also about the running?"

"Yes." She nodded her head hard. "Tomorrow. Ávrio. I'll find a way to explain to Mom and Yiayiá, and they'll talk to your *pappoús*." She raised his hand to her cheek, shaking her head. "I wish I could explain it to you better, because this is about *much* more than us being able to see each other. *So much more*. Anyway, no matter what—we have to *try*. *Prospatheí*, remember?"

He gazed at her, his eyes asking if she was serious. What he saw in her face made him smile, slow and sweet. "Yes," he said, "I remember."

Kat rushed down Yiayiá's lane, her whole body light and easy. She couldn't wait for tomorrow. Telling Mom and Yiayiá what she'd been up to would be bad, but if it meant they'd help straighten everything out with Kýrios Zafirakis, it would be worth it. Of course, she had no idea what they could say to change his mind, but . . . but hey, if she could run up a mountain, she could figure out a way to make the ancient fisherman understand, and make things right. If she could run up a mountain, she could figure out *lots* of things.

As she opened Yiayiá's gate, she glanced at her watch. 10:36 p.m. Yeorgia had to be freaking out by now.

"Where were you?" James jumped up from the table and blasted down the steps, Nikos close behind.

"Well, that's none of your business," she said, patting his head as she brushed by. "You guys should be in bed."

Nikos called to her, ending with "Yeorgia."

Kat whipped around. "What?"

"Where is Yeorgia?" said James, enunciating every word as if she'd gone deaf.

"What is this? Some kind of jo—" Her whole body went cold. The look on both James's and Nikos's faces told her Yeorgia was not there.

"We're not kidding. She's not here," said James. "She said you went for a dumb run, but you took too long and she had to find you and—Hey! Where are *you* going now? And what's with the flashlight?"

CHAPTER FORTY

Kat ran down the hill, whisper-yelling, "Yeorgia!" Her calls faded into the dark, unanswered.

She threw herself forward. *Come on, you have to be here. Have to be!* This was her fault. On her own, Yeorgia would never choose to go out alone after dark.

When she reached the beach, Kat stopped and scanned toward the town, searching for a solitary figure—probably beyond pissed off—walking along the road. She saw nothing. Nothing except a long, shadowy stretch of road sandwiched between black, silver-tipped sea and moonlit sky. She glared up at the moon, as if Artemis indeed listened from above. *You have to let Yeorgia be okay. You have to let me find her and get home.* Like a silvery, shadowy egg, it hovered, pale and remote as ever, and as Kat took off down the road again, another truth came clear. She was on her own.

Halfway to Paralia, she heard a racket in the distance ahead—a high-pitched whine. A motorbike, no, not one, at least two, maybe three.

The revving of engines rose and fell as though the bikes

moved toward her and away from her at the same time, a continuous, angry growl like wolves circling.

That's when she saw them down on the beach. Two motorbikes, darting in and out of the shadows in tight, lurching circles, their thin tires crunching and skidding. Trapped between them and the water was a girl, dashing one way, then the other.

"No!" Kat shouted, pouring on the speed, gripping her flashlight tight. If only it was a real weapon—a bow and arrow—*Artemis's bow and arrow.*

Then she saw another motorbike perched up on the road. Its rider watched the fright show, his head a huge, grotesque bobblehead.

Helmet-Man! Of course.

Spiky red heat filled her chest, burning everything away until there was only one thing left—fury.

CHAPTER FORTY-ONE

She ran toward him, at the same time pointing the flashlight and flicking it on. Bathed in a glaring beam, the bright blue of the motorbike made her falter. *Wait*—Helmet-Man's bike was old and chipped. She raised the flashlight and froze as two shocked eyes goggled at her from the black helmet's open visor.

"Manolis!"

Manolis twisted away, jerking up as he scrambled to kickstart his bike. She sprinted toward him.

"You stupid *vlákas!*" Swinging the flashlight like a hammer, she smacked his helmet. "I can't believe it was you. All this time."

"*Stamáta*, Katina. Stop!"

"I can't believe you painted your stupid bike to—to trick me." She cracked him again with the flashlight, shoving him. With a loud scraping *crunch*, he and his bike fell over, tumbling onto the beach.

"You are a stupid *vlákas*, Manolis. A stupid, *vlákas nýo nyo!*"

Even though she wanted more than anything to hit him again, instead she raced across the pebbles, holding her flashlight high as she ran between the still-circling bikes and Yeorgia.

"Efthimios, Michalis! Stop! Stop it, right now!"

She dove at the swooping bikes, and Yeorgia grabbed her hand, trying to pull her out of the way.

"No," Kat said, holding Yeorgia with her, refusing to give ground.

The bikes stopped, coming to rest side by side like gurgling beasts.

"*Éla*, Katina. What is the matter?" The words came out of their mouths slick and easy, as if they were all in the middle of an innocent game. "We have a little fun."

"A little *fun*? Is that what you jerks think?"

Kat waved at Yeorgia's face gleaming with tear streaks. "You think this is funny? That *she* thinks this is funny? You're scaring the *skatá* out of her."

"*Éla*. Is a joke." Now just Michalis spoke. "We are kidding." He called up to the road. "Manolis?"

"*Manolis?*" Yeorgia's whisper was a strangled choke, but when she whirled to the road her voice rang out, sharp and clear. "Manolis! *Éla!*"

Manolis scurried himself and his bike up to the road and, as if they were on the same team now, Michalis, Efthimios, and Yeorgia all shouted after him. Manolis yelled back then, three high-pitched, shrieking words over his shoulder, and kicking his bike to life, swooshed off into the night.

It's not me? The lameness of his parting had the others shouting at him even louder, but almost made Kat burst out laughing. Did he honestly think that because he wasn't down on the beach terrorizing Yeorgia with his idiot friends, he wasn't part of it? He'd gone too far this time. This time he would pay.

CHAPTER FORTY-TWO

With the roar of Manolis's bike fading into the night, Kat laid into Efthimios and Michalis again, only to be interrupted by the loud crunch of someone stomping across the beach. Someone who yelled Greek at them in a voice as jarring as trees thudding to the ground.

Kýrios Zafirakis.

Barely glancing at Yeorgia and Kat, he faced Michalis and Efthimios, continuing to scold.

"What's he saying?" Kat whispered to Yeorgia.

"He say he is walking home from the docks when he hear all this noise on the beach. This yelling. And he come to see." Yeorgia paused, listening more. "He say these boys behave badly. He will tell their parents."

Efthimios and Michalis circled their bikes toward the road, the tone of their mutterings bitter with how misunderstood their little joke was.

As they buzzed away, Kýrios Zafirakis spoke to Yeorgia, gentle now, and when he finished, Yeorgia turned to Kat. "Kýrios Zafirakis say he will walk us home. *Éla,*" she said, tugging at Kat's hand.

Kat didn't move. "Kýrios Zafirakis." She squeezed Yeorgia's hand, then let go and stepped forward to face him. "Wait, please."

She took a deep breath, glad it was too dark to see him clearly.

"*Efcharistó*," she said, pointing first to herself and then to Yeorgia. "Thank you, but—God, there's so much I want to say." She twisted to Yeorgia. "Help me, Yeorgia. How do I say that I feel bad that Theofilus and I were sneaking around, but-but that we only did it because he wouldn't let us see each other?"

She turned back to Kýrios Zafirakis. "And we *want* to see each other, but that's not really the point. He has to stop being so afraid and try to understand what Theofilus wants." She pulled her braid over her shoulder, worrying the ends. "He has to help him, with his art, his life. Because if he doesn't, *that's* what will make Theofilus leave Greece. Not some half-Greek American girl."

Yeorgia fed Kat the words, and even though the moonlight made everything indistinct, the steadiness of Kýrios Zafirakis's expression and the weight of his gaze told Kat he listened. That he heard her at last.

CHAPTER FORTY-THREE

"You are *so* kidding me." Kat finished tying her running shoe and glanced at Yeorgia, next to her on the swing. Even though a whole night and day had passed since the motorbike incident and subsequent family blowup, Yeorgia continued doling out tidbits from all the Greek that had been flying around. "What did Kýrios Zafirakis say?"

"He say he like how you got your Greek up," said Yeorgia, her smile a shy curve in the early-evening light. "When you are yelling. With Efthimios and Michalis. He say this is good. Very Greek."

They both cracked up, then Yeorgia's face went serious, and Kat twisted.

Yiayiá.

She cupped each girl's cheek before giving both of their heads a light cuff. "No more sneaking. Is no good."

"No more sneaking," both girls parroted.

"*Kalós,*" said Yiayiá, satisfied.

When she stepped back, Kat grabbed her hand. "Wait," she said, her eyes holding Yiayiá's, "I-I feel like ever since we got here, you've been trying to tell me stuff, about me, about the family, and I haven't really figured out this half-Greek thing, but I want to. I want to try. And the first thing I'm going to do is learn Greek. Then we can *really* talk." She turned to Yeorgia. "Will you please tell her what I said? That I mean it?"

Kat kept Yiayiá's hand as Yeorgia and Yiayiá spoke. Then Yeorgia turned to Kat.

"She say she know you come here wanting something. Looking for something. She know you will find this something. And she hope you are coming back to Greece. To this family. Like your mother. To come back here. Always she is here for you."

Yiayiá punctuated Yeorgia's words by patting her own chest.

"I know." Kat squeezed Yiayiá's hand. "*Efcharistó*, Yiayiá."

Yiayiá walked away, and Kat watched her for a moment before turning back to see that Yeorgia had taken the *tagári* onto her lap.

"I always like Artemis," Yeorgia said, stroking the wool before handing the bag to Kat. "She have good stories."

"Yeah. Unbelievable stories." Kat traced Artemis's profile with her finger. *Except*—her finger paused, her eyes lifting to the freshly risen moon, still huge even as it continued to wane—hadn't she *herself* been hunting? And what about all *her* protecting? Kat shook her head slightly, a whisper of laughter escaping between her lips. *Magic and not magic.* Maybe those stories weren't *that* unbelievable.

"I'd like to hear more about Artemis," Kat went on, smiling at Yeorgia as she put the bag down. "Mom brought this mongo book of Greek myths and—"

"This book?" Yeorgia's face lit. "It is in English?"

"Yeah."

"I would like to see this book."

"Hey, *I* know," Kat said, "how about you read it aloud to me?" She bumped Yeorgia's shoulder with her own. "You know, to practice your English?"

Yeorgia laughed and bumped Kat's shoulder back. "This make my mother very happy, and . . ." Her voice went low, mischievous. "I tell. About me and *pilótos*."

"You're kidding! What did she say?"

"I-I don't tell my *mamá* yet," said Yeorgia, her face beaming bright as a star. "I tell my *babás*, and he say, 'is good.' Soon, we tell her together."

"That's perfect." Kat stretched as she stood up. "I want the full story later, okay?"

A motorbike came to a rumbling stop outside Yiayiá's gate, and Kat sped down the steps.

Bike and biker sat in the lane, the gathering dark of early evening making the black helmet and visor gleam hard and shiny as the shell of a beetle.

"It's about time," called Kat.

"It took me a while to get the hang of this contraption," said Mom, flicking the visor up. "I could still use a couple more minutes with the gear shift." Her voice sounded light and easy, but her eyes, the only facial feature visible, still looked glazed from all the revelations of the past twenty-four hours.

Oh, well. At least Mom looked a lot happier than she did after getting home from last night's drinks party. Kat winced, remembering how Mom, Yiayiá, Theía Tassia, and Theíos Nick swung through the gate, happy and laughing, only to find Kýrios Zafirakis and Theofilus sitting at the table with her and Yeorgia.

The *skatá* had hit the fan: Theía Tassia going off in loud Greek, alternately flattening Yeorgia with hugs and shaking her by the arms, and Theíos Nick's face turning into a frowning stone as Kýrios Zafirakis spouted his part of the tale. For Kat, it was the silent hurt on Mom's face that made her want to bolt.

The only thing, or person rather, keeping her from doing that was Theofilus, sitting right beside her, holding her hand tight in his.

"I'm sorry." Kat must've said those words a gazillion times as she choked out the details about her nighttime running, about Theofilus—well, maybe not *everything* about him. At first Mom couldn't hear her, saying things like "I trusted you," and "I can't believe you were lying to me the whole time," until Kat was ready to explode.

"You didn't give me a choice!" Kat finally fired back. "I had to lie and—and I'm not sorry about wanting to be with Theofilus, or about wanting to run. I *told* you I wanted to run cross-country way before we came here. And I *told* you it was super important to me, but you wouldn't listen."

Mom's mouth opened, ready to dive back into the fray, but then Yiayiá put her hand on Mom's shoulder and whispered a few words that made Mom close her mouth and turn to Yiayiá with big, swimmy eyes. A moment later, Yiayiá and Mom squeezed each other in a tight hug.

"All right," Mom said, glancing back at Kat as she wiped her cheeks. "Yiayiá reminded me about a conversation I had with my dad a long time ago, and I'm not excusing what you did, but you're right. I didn't get how important your running was to you. I do now, though, and . . . I want to listen. I *am* listening."

And she did.

"Okay," said Mom. She took hold of the handlebars again. "I think I've got it."

"Are you sure you're up for this?" said Kat. She grinned.

"Hey, riding a motorbike could be great for your 'restart' rebellion-thingy."

"I don't know about that, but at least I'll be able to keep up with you while you run," Mom said, smile crinkles appearing at the corners of her eyes. "It's so generous of Kyría Marula to let us use the bike and helmet until the end of our stay."

After Manolis's antics the night before, Kyría Marula had taken the bike away from him, and promptly banished him back to Athens for the rest of the summer. He'd left hours ago on the morning bus.

Mom went on, "We'll have to make a point of thanking her again."

Before Kat could respond, the gate to Theía Tassia and Theíos Nick's cottage across the lane burst open, and James and Nikos all but fell through it.

"Mom," said James, "Theíos Nick is taking me and Nikos fishing with Kýrios Zafirakis tomorrow. We have to be at the docks by 5:00 a.m."

"Sounds good," said Mom. "You'd better go tell Yiayiá. I'm sure she'll want to organize a big picnic lunch for you to bring on the boat."

Hooting their excitement, the boys disappeared through Yiayiá's gate.

"So," said Mom, eyeing Kat, "if Nick and the boys are going fishing with Kýrios Zafirakis tomorrow, does that mean you and Theofilus get to start your *punishment?*"

"Probably." Kat avoided Mom's eyes by doing a side stretch.

"Although," Mom went on, "I really wonder if you two finishing painting Marula's shutters together *is* such a punishment."

"I'm sure it'll be pure misery," said Kat, keeping her face serious and stretching to the other side.

"Pure misery, huh?" Mom shook her head. "Would it be safe to say—all hijinks aside—coming to Paralia is working out better than you thought?"

"Yes," said Kat, straightening and looking Mom right in the eye. "It would be totally safe to say that."

"That makes me very happy, sweets. Okay then, are you ready to run?"

Kat gave her a thumbs-up and jogged down the road. And—*how weird was this?*—the sound of Mom chugging away on the motorbike behind her was downright comforting.

Breathing easily, Kat picked up her pace, and as she turned out of Yiayiá's lane, the twilight-blue glitter of the sea engulfed her, an endless wave of cheering friends. Then she was at the jetty, at the docks, and friends *were* cheering her on.

"*Éla*, Kat! *Brávo!*" Theofilus stood up high on the deck of his grandfather's boat, his arms punching the air. At the stern, Kýrios Zafirakis tipped his cap, offering a small salute. Without missing a step, Kat threw them a big smile and a quick wave. Running harder, she flew through the town, and there was Thula in front of the market. "*Yassou*, Katina!" she called, clapping her hands over her head. "Run!"

Kat kept going, everything in her juiced, electric. Yes, she loved the running, loved, loved, loved it.

When the road began to climb, her pace never wavered, each stride flowing fast and free. Tonight, she would run to the top of the mountain again, but maybe tomorrow she'd go in the complete opposite direction: run to the twin humps of land at the other end of the bay, visit the ruined temple. She glanced over her shoulder. For sure Mom would want to tell her all about it, every little Greek detail. Then perhaps the next day she'd go even farther down that road, see the Greece that spread beyond Paralia. Who knew what she'd discover there, maybe even another mountain.

After that? Images of Emma, Dad, high school, cross-country flitted through Kat's head: the possibilities of each a big, shiny question only she could answer. And wasn't *that* the best magic of all? The choice was hers.

The End

ACKNOWLEDGEMENTS

I am indebted to my big noisy American and Greek families. Many of them will recognize bits of themselves and their adventures in these pages. I want to thank chiefly and forever my mother Sofia, who let me read as much as I wanted, and never took a book away from me. I also want to express infinite appreciation for my *yiayiá* Kalomira. She couldn't speak much English to me, my brother, and my American cousins during all those Greek summers, but still she managed to share stories and jokes and so, so much of herself with us all.

Thank you to Vermont College of Fine Arts, particularly the MFA program in Writing for Children and Young Adults. My years in VCFA's enchanted bubble gave me the time, craft-knowledge, and community to write, and to believe I could write. Enormous gratitude and affection for my VCFA advisers: Uma Krishnaswami who nudged me to write something personal; Martine Leavitt who showed this book's first draft epic love, while simultaneously asking me the tough questions; Sharon Darrow who encouraged me to explore my characters' feelings more fully; and Tim Wynne-Jones who shepherded this book through revisions with precision and care, challenging me to dig deeply into motivation, plot, and action. Each of you owns a piece of my writer's heart. A special nod to my VCFA class, The Sweet Dreams and Flying Machines. Our time together was a true gift. Extra love and thanks to Sweet Dreamers Jess Dils and Daphne Kalmar. Lucky, lucky me to have shared the past fifteen or so years with you two as my best and closest writing buddies, critique partners, cheerleaders, and pals. Also, a shout-out to Tanya Lee Stone who taught me heaps about writing for children, and was the one who told me about VCFA in the first place.

Tremendous thanks to all the early champions and readers of the manuscript—too many to name here—please, please know that my gratitude is boundless. Express thanks to Erzsi Deák who plucked Kat and her story out of the slush pile and gave me and this manuscript time, professional advice, and productive feedback. And appreciation to Miriam Altshuler and Ginger Knowlton. Each of you provided spot-on critiques that were invaluable in helping me make this book better.

Major gratitude to SparkPress without whom this book would not exist. My hat is off to publisher Brooke Warner and to the entire SparkPress team for collaborating with me on making a beautiful book. Deep appreciation to writing pal Kathy Elkind, whose experience with She Writes Press—Spark's sister imprint—made me believe my book could at last find a home, and to fellow Sparks Kristin Nilsen and Cindy Callaghan, who offered the kind of support, information, and encouragement that had me taking the plunge.

And last—but never least—huge love and bottomless appreciation for my most important and needed supporters. My husband Charlie, who over our entire marriage has talked books and writing with me tirelessly, along with reading and critiquing my writing (plus building me my amazing whimsy wagon!). And our three children: Jack, Willy, and Marley, who since their earliest days have inspired me, read with me, talked stories with me, as well as giving critique and suggestions about not only this story in particular, but also so many more. *Efcharistó polý*, and I love you forever.

ABOUT THE AUTHOR

Mima Tipper is half Greek and half American, and her writing reflects her heritage—a little bit old-country, a little bit rock and roll; one foot wandering through the dreamy realm of myths and faerie tales, the other running on the solid ground of fast-paced, contemporary story. She earned her MFA in Writing for Children and Young Adults from Vermont College of Fine Arts, and has published YA fiction in *Hunger Mountain* and *Sucker Literary Magazine*. When not working on her own writing, she is committed to promoting literacy and to supporting the writing community. Mima lives in Vermont.

Please visit Mima at mimatipper.com

Looking for your next great read?

We can help!

Visit www.gosparkpress.com/next-read
or scan the QR code below for a list
of our recommended titles.

SparkPress is an independent boutique publisher
delivering high-quality, entertaining, and engaging
content that enhances readers' lives, with a special
focus on commercial and genre fiction.